D1189610

THE GHOST
BETWEEN US

PETE NUNWEILER

Dedication

This is dedicated to all those dealing with their own ghosts of the past. Some of us are lonely, sitting around an empty home, imagining someone else sitting next to us watching a movie together. Others of us are suffering from a broken heart after a relationship that ended too soon. If we think about that person hard enough, we can still see them, hear their laughter and smell their scent, but they're completely out of reach and we can't feel them. Then many of us still recall vivid memories of times spent with someone who has passed on.

We are all haunted by our ghosts of the past. Embrace them, for they have shaped us and they truly are our memories of once upon a time.

Prologue

Memories of Once Upon a Time

I awake to my alarm in the morning, the radio playing your favorite artist.
The morning's tough, midday's ok, but it's the nighttime that is the hardest.

The ghost of a memory still in my room, the sweet smell of perfume in the air.
Your body laying against my skin, a soft whisper rings clear in my ear.

I pull my pillow much closer to me in hopes that the feeling will do.
I'm a fool to think that anything could come close to replacing you.

I try again to toss and to turn, trying to shake the memory away.
But you've etched a place into my heart, and that's where I want you to stay.

I turn over and find that another ghost is lying on that side too,
Looking and smiling with beautiful eyes, an image that still seems so new.

I cuddle with you and drift off to sleep, wake in the morning to your favorite artist.
The morning's tough, midday's ok, but it's the nighttime that is the hardest.

Your ghost returns with a beautiful smile, your eyes sparkle like charms.
You lay again against my skin and I welcome you with open arms.

~Tobias Miller

I froze when I heard the news. I couldn't believe it. I was stunned into silence; truly shocked. My heart sank as my back hit the wall with a thud, my knees buckled, and I slowly slid down the wall. My knees met my chest with the phone still pressed to my ear.

I hung up the phone with Anna just twenty minutes before. She called to tell me she was on her way home from a girls' night out. I smiled during the whole conversation and paced while we talked as I teased her about the rest of the night I had planned for her.

"Hope you're not too tired," I said, as I stood by the entryway admiring the atmosphere I had created for her. I needed to see it just as she would when she got home. The entire living room was dimly lit by ten candles; one representing each year of our marriage. Shadows of trinkets silently danced across the walls and tables. There was a candle by the front door, one on each of the two bookcases I built by the fireplace. There was one on each end of the mantle, one on the coffee table, one on the dining room table, one on the granite countertop in the kitchen and two in the bedroom. Every opposite candle had a different scent, starting with lavender and ending with peppermint. I had just finished walking through the house to make sure everything was perfect.

In the bedroom, her black, satin chemise was laid out on the bed next to the matching robe; a perfect contrast to her long blonde hair. There was a hand towel on the nightstand with peppermint massage oil next to it. I left the bedroom and walked down the short hallway to the large opening of the dining room to the left and living room to the right.

In the living room, the square, dark wood coffee table had a white cloth laid across it like a diamond, with the corners slightly hanging over each side. There was a tray of sliced bananas, marshmallows, pieces of angel food cake, strawberries and warm chocolate in a small fondue pot. The two skewers were displayed perfectly in front of the warm pot of chocolate.

I turned the thermostat down to sixty-seven degrees, knowing that the candles and the gas fireplace would warm the entire downstairs. The soft music of our favorite playlist made us think of relaxing on either our own back porch, or the ones we had enjoyed during our trips to the Tennessee mountains so many times.

"Oh, I'm not too tired," she replied.

"Good, because I'm going to keep you up for a very long time."

"What do you have planned?" she asked with an anticipating smile.

"Really? You truly think I'm going to tell you?" I asked.

"After fourteen years together, you know I'm going to keep trying. What's the occasion?"

I laughed and said, "Does there have to be an occasion?" which was more of a statement than a question. "It's Saturday. You're the most beautiful girl in the world and I want to spoil you. That's the occasion."

"Don't be an ass all your life, Toby," she laughed.

"Oh c'mon, please? Just for tonight at least?" I mocked, then asked how her night out with the girls was.

"Oh, it was fun, as always. Lots of laughter over an awesome meal. My face hurts every time we get together from the four of us laughing so hard."

"That's great, baby. I'm glad you had a good time."

"It's started to snow." She told me. "It's blowing around like I'm in a snow globe. It's really pretty even though I'm getting sick of it. It's March, for Christ's sake, I'm ready for Spring"

I smiled without replying and she asked, "How are the book ideas coming along? Did you come up with anything?"

"Nothing. I jotted some things down, but nothing is jumping out at me."

"There's no rush and you don't need to force an idea. Maybe it would be better if you let it come to you instead of chasing after a plot."

"I can't wait for you to come home and see what's

in store for you." I said.

"Don't you change the subject on me!" she demanded with a playful giggle.

"I just get discouraged sometimes since I'm not getting much of an audience with my first book. I'm sure that makes my boss happy because I won't be retiring any time soon."

I was silent for a moment and stopped pacing before telling her, "I sure do love you, sweetheart. I'm really excited for you to come home."

"I love you too, baby, and you've certainly made me excited to get home."

"You have no idea," I smirked.

I thought about the blowing snow and changed my tone when I said, "Be careful, honey. I'll see you in a little while."

"I will. See you soon, baby. I love you."

"I love you too, Anna."

I crouched on the tile floor of the dining room with the phone clutched tightly in my hand and shook my head in disbelief.

"Sir? Sir! Are you still there?" the officer asked.

"Yes," I whispered.

"We've called to have her airlifted to Community Hospital. They're on their way now."

"Is—is she alive?"

"She is right now, sir. They're doing everything they can. EMTs will accompany her at all times."

"Okay," was all I could say.

"I'm so sorry, sir. I'll personally let her know she'll see you soon."

The phone disconnected before I could end the call. I looked around the house in the deafening silence, still staring in disbelief with the words repeating in my head from the second call I answered from Anna's phone.

> *"Hey, baby, did you miss me that much that you had to call again before you got home?"*
>
> *But it wasn't my wife. A man's voice responded. "Tobias Miller?"*
>
> *"Yes, who's this?"*
>
> *"This is officer Sean Carter. You're listed on a cell phone as an ICE contact. What is your relationship with Annaliese Miller?"*
>
> *"She's my wife."*
>
> *"Sir, your wife's been in an accident."*
>
> *I listened intently as Officer Carter continued, "The ambulance just arrived and they're doing everything they can for her."*
>
> *"What do you mean they're doing everything they can for her? What happened?"*
>
> *"She's been in an accident, sir. Best we can tell, a truck entered the curve at 82nd and Sargent Rd., crossed the center line and lost control. She was struck directly and her car was pushed off the road and turned upside down. Sir? Sir! Are you still*

there?"

I stood up slowly, put my phone on the counter and heard a low-flying helicopter overhead, so I looked at the ceiling, following the sound from one end to the other. My mind began to process the news the best it could. What did he mean by *"She's alive right now?"* I moved quickly through the house, turned off the music, blew out each jar candle and turned off the gas fireplace. I changed out of my black, silk boxers into appropriate clothing, and grabbed my keys and phone off the kitchen granite.

After I sped out of the garage in the two-year-old Sorento and drove away from the house, my imagination raced with possibilities; each one worse than the previous.

She's been knocked unconscious and will be fine when I get to the hospital. But they wouldn't call for her to be airlifted if she's been knocked unconscious. So, what the hell do they know? They've made a mistake. Maybe she wasn't wearing her seatbelt and her head went through the windshield. Was she just lying there on the hood? She couldn't have been; they said the car was upside down. Was she crushed? Maybe she's got cuts all over her. Maybe she's bleeding out somewhere. Oh shit. What if I don't make it to the hospital on time? I'm going to get there and pace in the waiting room for twenty minutes just for some doctor to come in, take his hair net off, lower his head and ask me to take a seat just to tell me he did all he could do, but she didn't make it.

I shook off the thoughts and returned my focus to the road. I descended the hill towards Fall Creek Road. The light was green, so I went straight through and climbed the curvy hill on the other side. Thick woods lined each side of the road and there was no one else driving in either direction. I heard the roar of helicopter rotors and my heart sank once again. With a heavy sigh, I fought back anxious tears. I watched the flashing lights of the helicopter lift into the night air. The lights got smaller and the sound faded as it sped into the distance and I realized exactly where I was. I was on 82nd Street approaching the bend and the traffic light at Sargent Road. I let off the gas and slowly eased my brakes when I saw flashes of red, yellow and blue off the trees ahead. The lights were blinding as I neared the bend. I squinted and focused on the lines of the road. There was an officer directing me to stay to the right. My heart raced and I tried to focus entirely on the directions of the officer and the lines on the road amid the flashing lights. I turned just my eyes to the left without realizing what I had done. Oh, how I loathed the sight. Through a flood of tears and the blinding flashes of red, blue and yellow off the falling snow, I saw the underside of my wife's car. Thick black tire marks led to the pickup truck that was traveling in the opposite direction; the front end completely ripped off.

Firefighters were moving around the scene, taking pictures, jotting notes, crouching on the ground to look inside the inverted car and briefly talking to each other. There was a large, blue tarp draped over the driver's side of the truck. Next to the tarp, two men crouched upon the ground briefly and simultaneously lifted each end of a gurney with a long black bag on top of it, extending the legs until they locked. I gasped because I knew exactly what was in that black bag. That's when something else caught my attention. A detail that I will never forget as long as I'm alive.

Inside the bed of the truck, I saw a man. He wore a thick dark winter coat and wasn't at all bothered by the bitter cold. He had a ball cap on his head. His hands were covering his face completely and his shoulders shook from sobbing. As I passed, he pulled his face from his hands, slowly turned his eyes to me and without a sound, said, "I'm so sorry."

No one was tending to him or even cared that he was sitting in the middle of the scene of the accident. They all moved about as though he didn't exist at all. I braked harder to stop the SUV.

"Keep it moving" I heard one of the officers yell. As I approached him, I lowered my window so that I could ask about the man in the back of the truck. Just as I opened my mouth to speak, I glanced back at the bed of the truck. It was empty.

"Sir, please keep moving," the officer repeated. I stared up at him as competing emotions were now racing through me.

"Please, sir," he said one more time.

I turned my attention back to the road, rounded the bend and sped forward when the road straightened. For the first time in years, I turned to a stranger to ask for help.

"Please, God, give her a chance. Please don't take her from me."

I turned into the complex of Community Hospitals and sped along the winding access roads until I reached the parking lot closest to the emergency entrance. I threw the truck into Park, unfastened my seatbelt and opened the door in what seemed like a single swift motion. I ran up to the entrance and impatiently waited for the two sets of automatic doors to open, then ran inside to the front desk.

"I'm here to see my wife, Annaliese Miller," I announced to the two ladies behind the desk.

"Tobias Miller?" I heard a deep voice respond from behind me.

I turned to see the police officer who called out my name and approached him. He was a bald, stalky man, standing more than six feet tall. I walked over to him anxiously wiping away stray tears from my cheeks. He reached his hand out and I saw his nametag before he could introduce himself; CARTER

"I'm Officer Sean Carter. I'm the one who called about your wife's accident."

Chapter 1

Reflections

"How is she? Is she still—"

"Yes, she's still here," he interrupted. "They took her to the Neuro ICU. I'll take you to the waiting room. They're still getting her settled, but you can wait there until they're ready for you."

"Can I ask you some questions?" I requested.

"Sure, I'll answer what I can, but I don't know anything about her condition.

I got right to the point, "What happened?"

"She was driving East on 82nd Street through the intersection at Sargent Road. Are you familiar with that intersection?"

"Yes," I told him. "I drive it every day."

"She crossed Sargent and started into the left curve when a guy in a pickup truck was driving Westbound too fast to handle the curve approaching the intersection. He hit the front corner of your wife's car on the driver's side. The impact rolled the car upside down."

"Is that the official police report? How sure are you of what happened?"

"I saw it happen, Mr. Miller. I was driving North on Sargent and had the red light at the intersection. I heard the screeching of tires and looked up just after your wife passed through the intersection. There was nothing she could do to avoid it."

"Was she trapped? Did she have her seat belt on? I mean, what's she like?" I drilled.

"She had her seat belt on, which saved her life. She has a couple of cuts on her arm and one on the side of her head where it slammed against the door jamb from the impact."

I sighed and said, "So, it's not all that serious—good."

"Sir, she hit her head pretty hard. You have to understand we estimate the truck was going more than forty miles an hour at the time of impact. Your wife is lucky to be alive. If she was a fraction of a second faster, the truck would have hit her door and I'm quite certain we would be having a different conversation."

We had reached the waiting room and he held the door for me to enter. I sat down and put my head in my hands with my elbows on my knees. Officer Carter sat across from me and placed his hat on his knee.

"So, now what?" I asked.

"I wish I knew, Mr. Miller."

"Please, it's Toby," I said.

I paused as I replayed the events that were just explained to me in my mind.

"You were the first one there, weren't you, Officer Carter?"

"Please, call me Sean, and yes, I got to your wife first. She was unconscious, which could be a blessing. The mind just can't process events like that."

"I don't understand," I began. "She was hit at forty miles an hour, the car was turned upside down, she doesn't have any significant bleeding, yet she had to be airlifted.

"When the EMTs arrived, they looked her over. It was their decision to make. Toby, a head injury is nothing to play with. What you don't see could be worse than what you can."

I contemplated even asking the next question since I already knew the answer, but I needed to hear it for myself.

I took a deep breath and blurted out, "And what about the other driver?"

Sean looked down at the floor between his knees, sighed and shook his head. He finally looked up at me and said, "He didn't make it. He um—he was ejected from the truck. I found him about thirty-five feet into the field there."

"Sean, what was he wearing?" I asked.

"Man, I can't—I—he was—look, I don't know if his family has been contacted yet. I can't tell you about him, I'm sorry."

"I'm not asking details about the man himself, just curious. What was he wearing?" I asked.

"He had on work boots, jeans, a thick navy-blue coat and a ball cap. Why? Do you know him?"

I leaned back in my chair and closed my eyes remembering the man I saw in the bed of the pickup truck.

"Mr. Miller, do you know him?"

"No. It's just odd, isn't it, Officer. Two people at the same place, at the same time in the same situation and one is airlifted to the hospital while the other lays lifeless in the field."

Officer Carter must have found irony in that statement. He briefly laughed and shook his head, then said, "I've asked myself that more times than I can count."

"Why are you here?" I asked him.

"Toby, an officer's job doesn't end with speeding tickets and catching bad guys. Not to me anyway."

His radio squelched and a voice called out, "Dispatch to twenty-seven forty-four."

He reached for the button on the side of the microphone hooked onto his shoulder, "Twenty-seven forty-four, go ahead."

He stood up, walked over to me and extended his hand before the woman responded to him again.

"You alright?" he asked.

I tried to stand, but he insisted that I didn't need to get up.

"No, sir, I'm not alright at all," I said. "Not until I know Anna's okay."

He pulled a pen and a notepad from his pocket and started writing as he said, "Here, this is my personal cell phone number. If there's anything at all I can do, please don't hesitate to call."

"Dispatch to twenty-seven forty-four" the radio sounded again.

Sean looked at me with a puzzled, yet disgusted look, pushed the button on his mic again and spoke very slowly, "Twenty-seven forty-four, go ahead," and shook his head. He reached down and grabbed my shoulder before turning to walk out the glass doors.

I stood up again and walked towards a wall of windows, opposite from the doors to the waiting room, but saw more of my own reflection than anything outside in the darkness.

I paced in the waiting room anxiously glancing every time I saw a doctor or nurse walk by. There was a small station set up with coffee and water in one corner. Another area had a stand with informational pamphlets for diabetes, sleep apnea, STDs, how to quit smoking, heart conditions, signs of concussions and some for brain-related things that I could hardly pronounce. I walked the length of the waiting room one more time until I reached a corner seat that would offer me a view of the entire room and sat down again.

I had never felt as alone as I did at that moment. Even when Anna and I were apart, I never felt alone. I had her, she had me. That's just the way it was. I felt lost; lost in myself, lost in the situation. I felt helpless. Somewhere through another set of double doors, my Anna was lying in a hospital bed and there was absolutely nothing I could do to help her, support her or even just tell her again how much I love her. I scanned the room again, seemingly, for answers; answers that would never come. I stood up again and walked to the opposite corner of the room, just to be closer to the double doors into the ICU and closer to Anna. I stood as still as a statue and focused all of my attention on my sense of hearing, but no sounds were reaching me. I lapped the room on the outside of the rows of chairs with my fingers interlaced on the crown of my head looking at the ceiling, then back to the floor until I reached my corner seat again and sat down. *How long am I going to have to wait,* I thought to myself. *Why isn't anyone coming? Is she waking up? Is she still alive? What's happening in that room back there?* The doors to the waiting room opened and I quickly stood up to see who it was. She wore a blue hospital gown.

"Ma'am, can you tell me anything about Annaliese Miller?"

"I'm sorry, sir, I'm just changing out the coffee," she said.

I walked back over to the window wall to the outside. There was still a light snow falling. The wind seemed to stop because the flakes were falling straight down now. I focused my eyes away from the snow and onto my own reflection.

Do you have what it takes? Can you handle this at all? I looked myself in the eyes as I reflected on each question but couldn't answer either one of them. *What do you see?* I saw fear. I saw anxiety. I saw confusion. I focused back to the snow and ignored the man in the reflection. I couldn't help him any more than I could help Anna. I turned my back on him and sat down in my corner seat just as the coffee started brewing and the woman left the waiting room.

Other than the gurgling coffee pot, the only sound in the room was my own rhythmic breathing. I breathed more deeply than usual, taking a moment to be thankful for the chance to be breathing at all. I placed my left hand on my heart just to feel it beating. I closed my eyes in gratitude for life itself; something I had taken for granted until just that moment. The thoughts in my head slowly cleared until my breathing regulated, my heartbeat slowed, and I focused on the chair I sat in and the room that surrounded me. The doors to the waiting room opened and a doctor walked through.

"Mr. Miller?" he said as I stood once again.

"Yes."

"I'm Anna's Doctor. She goes by Anna, right?"

"Yes, she does."

"Look, I'm going to get straight to it here, okay? Your wife has a fractured skull, resulting in a TBI, or traumatic brain injury, along with a subdural hematoma, which is pooling of blood between her brain and her skull."

"How is she? Can I see her? Is she going to make it?"

"She's sedated, and we'll be monitoring her around the clock until her situation changes," he said. "The hematoma is causing a lot of pressure on the brain. Keeping her sedated will help reduce the swelling and reduce the chances for more damage to her brain."

"So, she's going to make it?" I asked.

"Mr. Miller, it's early. We take the status of brain injuries as we see them. If the swelling gets bad enough, I may need to remove a small portion of her skull to ease the pressure."

"Her goddamn skull? Are you serious?"

"Sir, I need to make this as plain as I can. The pressure on her brain can become life-threatening. As I said, we're monitoring her every move."

"When will we know that she's okay?" I asked.

"I can't answer that, Mr. Miller. We just don't know."

"What about the rest of her? Does she have any cuts, bruises or anything broken?"

"She has some minor cuts on the left side of her body, none that would need sutures, and a hairline fracture in her ulna," he said and pointed to the outside of his arm between his elbow and wrist. "Believe me, those are the least of your worries," he continued.

"Where—when do I—how long—" I stumbled over every word until I finally told him, "I just don't know what to ask or what to say.

I don't understand, and I don't know how to understand."

"Mr. Miller—"

"Toby," I interrupted.

He took a breath and said, "Toby, the brain controls everything in the body.   Not just memory or cognitive thought, but body temperature, sense of time, when we're hungry, when we're full. Everything that our body does or reacts to is because of signals sent to and from the brain. It may be a few days before we really know the extent of any damage to hers."

"Can I see her?" I asked.

"I'd like to wait another couple of hours before I let you see her. These first few hours with a brain injury are vital. If you want to come back in the morning, we can reevaluate then."

"I'm not fucking leaving. Which is it? A couple of hours or overnight?" I demanded.

"I'm sorry, Mr. Miller, that's not what I meant. As long as there are no surprises, I'll let you see her every two hours for fifteen minutes starting at" —he looked at the clock on the wall and continued— "1:30 a.m. If you live close and want to get anything from your home, I can call you if there's any change in her condition before 1:30."

I looked away from him and considered the options.

He continued, "You don't have to answer that. All in due time. I'll come out here at 1:30 and if you're not here, I'll call. How does that sound?"

I nodded my head in agreement and he offered his right hand. I reached mine out to meet his and he placed his left hand on my shoulder, looked me in the eye and said, "Toby, I'm sorry as hell about your wife's accident. There's no one I trust more than the staff here. I promise you we'll do everything we can."

He shook my hand once and turned towards the doors.

"Oh, I almost forgot," he turned around to address me again. "there's some paperwork we'll need you to complete. I'll have a nurse bring it to you. If you decide to go home, please complete the paperwork first so I know how to get a hold of you."

"Thanks, Doc." I said.

He walked out the double doors of the waiting room, entered a code on the wall and went through another set of doors. I walked back over to the window once again and stared into the darkness. The fresh layer of snow reflected the lights of the buildings, parking lots and streets all around, making the night glow like dusk. There were rings around the street lights from the snowy mist.

I still felt alone. I still felt fear, anxiety, and confusion. I fixed my gaze back onto my reflection. The man I stared at now looked somewhat different. He stood a little straighter. He was slightly more confident and a bit stronger; a facade he would have to maintain for as long as it was possible.

Chapter 2

You Have to Fight

I turned away from the window and sat on the edge of my corner seat. I leaned against the back and crossed my legs with my hands folded across my stomach. My mind raced but I tried to focus on the one thing I *could* do in that moment. I had a task; a responsibility. There was finally something I could do.

I heard the doors open and a nurse walked in with a clipboard. There was a form for medical history, several consent forms and the one that I didn't know how to answer; a DNR form.

Do Not Resuscitate? How can I answer that? We've never discussed anything like this. In the event of an organ failure, does she want lifesaving procedures to be performed or is her wish just to let her go?

"Fuck that. Bring her back," I said under my breath as I flipped to the next form.

"Excuse me, sir?" the nurse said aloud. I hadn't realized she was waiting for me.

"Sorry, Ma'am, I just don't have the answer to this and, without that knowledge, I have to give her the opportunity to make that decision herself by not completing it."

I looked up at her for approval, but she had no reaction.

"Can I think about this for a little while?" I asked.

"I'm sorry, sir, but—uh—I really need—sir, you can complete the rest of the paperwork first while you think about it, but I really need all of it completed right away."

"Why? Did something happen?" I inquired.

"No, sir, it's just that with a head injury, things could change in an instant."

I looked down at the pamphlet provided with the DNR order so I could determine if I should fill it out or not. It listed reasons that someone would choose to complete it, just as there were reasons listed that someone would not. I saw phrases like "Quality of Life," "Aggressive Interventions," and "Natural, Peaceful Death."

What would she want? If there's no chance for a quality of life, why hang on? Who determines what quality of life she'll have? They'll still try something, according to the pamphlet, just not for a long time. There are risks of broken ribs and punctured organs. Is that what they mean by aggressive measures?

All of those thoughts ran through my mind over and over. I kept telling myself that if her heart stops, they'll still try to bring her back, but not for an extended amount of time. I completed the form last and turned the clipboard back to the nurse. She tucked it under her arm and walked out through the glass doors as though she was in a relay race with someone waiting down the hallway for their turn to carry it on.

What have I done?

It was 11:52 p.m., according to my phone; more than an hour and a half before I could see Anna, and I was feeling overwhelmed again. I had felt like this before in my life and knew what I had to do. I needed a way to turn the emotions into facts by keeping a journal of events. That way, all of the information I gathered was on my computer and not in my head.

I looked around the room again, but my thoughts extended beyond the walls. Where was I? Where was the parking lot? Where was my truck? I didn't have the luxury of taking a lot of time to make a decision. Every minute counted; every second counted.

I got my bearings, glanced at the clock one more time and briskly walked out the glass doors, down each corridor and out of the emergency room doors. As soon as I passed through the second set of double doors, I broke out into a run until I reached my truck. Just as I raced to get to the hospital, I raced to get home to gather a few things. The intersection of 82nd and Sargent was clear except the broken guard rail where Anna's car had crashed just a couple of hours before. The black tire marks were glossed over by the sheen of the wet road.

As I got close to the house, I pushed the button on the rear-view mirror to open the garage door. I was still out of range, but never took my finger off the button until I saw the light break through the bottom of the door when it began to lift.

When I parked, I ran into the house and grabbed my iPad, laptop, wireless headset, chargers to go with all of them and placed them all in my black backpack. I passed the fridge, grabbed a couple of Diet Mountain Dew cans, added them to the pack and started back towards the garage when a flickering light in the living room caught my eye. I slowly walked into the room to see a single candle by the front door still lit; the flame barely catching a draft in the air, directing shadows like a conductor swaying to a masterpiece.

I walked towards the candle, with one strap of the backpack over my left shoulder, and stared at it for a moment, then scanned the entire room. The once romantic setting looked dark. The fireplace was cold and a tray of food with a fondue pot was still staged on the coffee table. My imagination began again.

> *The candles and fireplace slowly relit themselves. I saw the ghost of myself enter the living room from the small hallway leading from the bedroom, looking around with a smile. He crouched on the floor between the couch and the coffee table in his black, silk boxers. The door opened behind me and Anna walked through. She closed the door, unzipped her coat, turned around and covered her mouth with a gasp. She was so beautiful with her tall boots, black leggings, and cream-colored sweater. She removed the scarf from around her neck and hung it over her coat.*
>
> *"Oh, my God, Baby, it's perfect."*
>
> *My ghost smiled bigger and stood up to embrace her. I walked around them to see her face. As I circled around them a second time, blood started to flow from the left side of her head. There were cuts up her arm. I closed my eyes tightly and denied my*

imagination to think like that any longer.

I stared, once again at a cold, dark room. I turned to blow out the candle and walked towards the garage again, threw my backpack on the passenger seat, started the truck and backed out of the driveway again. I shifted to Drive and looked at the clock; 12:19 a.m.

I got back to the waiting room with forty-seven minutes to spare. I pulled a drink and my laptop out of my backpack, turned the computer on and waited for it to boot. I entered my password, opened a new document and began to write. When I finished capturing the events of the night, I closed my laptop and looked around the room. There was a small monitor by the corner of the ceiling that wasn't on before, with a bar across the top displaying the word VISITATION. Underneath the bar was a single line, A. MILLER. *What does that mean?*

The glass doors opened, and her doctor greeted me with a smile.

"Mr. Mill—" he stopped himself and smiled. "Sorry about that. Toby."

"What do you say, Doc?" I said confidently as I stood and shook his hand.

"You can see her now," he said with a smile. He pointed to the monitor and continued, "In the future, when we're ready for you, her name will display up there, just like it's showing now."

"When is the next time I'll get to see her then, 3:30 or 3:45 since I'm taking up fifteen minutes now?" I asked.

"It will always be on the half hour."

He started walking away and I followed.

"Toby, this is sometimes pretty tough to see. Anna is sedated and

24

there are a lot of machines. She's intubated, and I have her connected to a cranial monitor that's on the front left side of her head."

"Is she stable?"

I didn't know what I was asking, it's just something I've heard people ask on TV and it sounded like it was a good thing.

He stopped, turned to me and said, "She's in Neuro Intensive Care for a reason. There's nothing stable about her condition right now. That's why we're monitoring everything."

I stared at him stone-faced.

He continued with, "I'll explain everything when we get there."

We turned a corner to the left and when he reached the third room on the right, he pushed the curtain away and walked through. I followed him in, pushing the curtain away myself.

Nothing could have prepared me for what I saw. My eyes welled up with tears. My lip curled, barely a moment before the sobs began. I tried to speak, but all that came out was a high-pitched whimper, "Anna. Oh, God, Anna."

Her eyes were blackened and swollen shut. There was a thin rod piercing into her head on the front-left side and there was a temporary cast on her left arm. Her mouth gaped open around the intubation tube. The sounds; oh God, the sounds. With a click, a gush of air and another click, I watched her chest rise. Click, whoosh, click, and it fell again. Beep—beep—beep beep—beep beep—beep—beep. The heart monitor and brainwave monitor sounded off with different tempos. I walked closer to the bed with Anna on my right and placed my hand on her leg just as I heard a gentle, low roar of a motor like an automated air mattress. Something on her leg was expanding. I removed my hand and looked at the doctor who stood in the corner watching me respectfully.

"They're sequential compression devices. They help with blood flow to the legs. We just call them leg wraps."

I turned back to Anna staring at her eyes like some gruesome movie that I couldn't look away from.

"What happened to her eyes?" I asked as I began to gain control of my sobbing.

"The impact of the accident caused her brain to hit against the inside of her skull. It's common with injuries like this."

I placed my palm ever so gently on the left side of her face and I felt a hand on my back between my shoulder blades.

"Are you okay?" Doc asked.

Without turning away from her, I whispered, "I don't know what I expected, but I certainly didn't expect this."

Doc reached over and pointed to the thin rod coming out of her head.

"This," he said, "is the cranial monitor. It measures the amount of pressure on her skull. These," he continued as he pointed to several things connected to her head, "monitor her brain activity that I can see on this screen here."

I turned to look at the screen.

"We're also monitoring her blood pressure, her heart rate, her oxygen lev—"

"Stop," I whispered. "What are we looking at here, Doc? How bad is she?"

"Toby, she's really bad. I'm showing you these things so you know that we are alerted, instantly, if there's any change at all." He paused. "I can't imagine how hard it is to only see her for fifteen minutes every two hours, but please understand, she needs to rest. It's the only hope for healing the brain."

"Can I have a minute, please?"

He thought about it for a moment and said, "I'll be right out here."

He pulled the curtain shut behind him.

I took Anna's hand in mine. I looked at her, then looked at the machines, then back at her again as I conjured the best smile I could.

"Hi, Sweetheart. It's me. You got into a hell of a mess, didn't you? It will be okay, baby. Just promise me you'll fight. This might be the hardest thing you've ever done, but you must fight this, sweetheart."

I pulled her hand up to my lips and kissed the back of her hand.

"We have so much left to do. We have to quit our jobs and work at the sock store in the mountains, remember? We have to go on the Alaskan Cruise to see the whales. We need to photograph the waterfalls of Iceland and," I swallowed hard. "you need to take me to the Pacific Northwest to see Mount Rainier and Mount Hood; Mount Saint Helens and Multnomah Falls. Baby, we need to spend the night at the old sanitarium in Louisville and I need to take you to the Stanley Hotel in Colorado."

Though tears continued to fall, I began to laugh lightly.

"Not that I'll ever sleep again when we go to those places. Remember when I saw the apparition running across the Peach Orchard at Gettysburg? Holy shit, I was so scared. We had to get you a new crystal before we went to any more haunted places.

Remember? Mary at the Cashtown Inn took yours. We have the dowsing rods and the spirit box still. We can take those to the Sanitarium when we go since we've had luck with them."

I wiped silent tears from my eyes, then rubbed my fingers gently through her hair that laid on her chest.

"Baby, it's almost time for me to go, but I won't be far. I'll be just out in the waiting room, okay, baby? I'll see you in two hours. I love you, sweetheart. I love you so much."

I kissed her hand with each statement.

"I'll see you soon, baby. You keep fighting, okay? You keep fighting, sweetheart. You *have* to fight."

Doc came in and I stepped around the curtain, out of her room.

"Can you find your way back?" he asked.

Still looking at Anna, I leaned with the curtains as he closed them to see her for as long as possible.

"What?" I said since I didn't hear a word he said, but knew he had spoken.

"Can you find your way back to the waiting room?"

"Uh, no, I really don't think I have any idea how we got here."

He said something into his communication radio that I didn't really hear, but I think he called for someone to sit with Anna. We walked down the hallway, through a set of double doors and the waiting room was immediately on the right side.

"Wow. It felt like a lot longer going the other way." I said. "Doc, how do I get back in when her name shows up on the monitor again?"

"There's a keypad on the wall. The five-digit code is 21244. Please don't come back until you're called."

"I understand." I told him as I walked through the glass doors into the waiting room and sat in my corner seat. I leaned back in my chair with visions of Anna burned into my mind. I pulled out my laptop and updated the journal, yawing with every bullet point I typed. When I was finished, I closed my laptop and tucked it away into the backpack. My drink was still on the table next to my chair. I leaned back again, folded my hands across my stomach and closed my eyes.

Chapter 3

Alone

"Mr. Miller? Mr. Miller."

I felt someone shaking my arm.

"Tobias Miller."

I snapped out of my sleep and instantly looked at the monitor. Her name was not showing. It was 6:15.

I snapped, "Why didn't someone come get me for my visitation?"

"Mr. Miller, you need to come with me," said the nurse that I hadn't seen before. She was a short girl with pale skin and short auburn hair. I grabbed my backpack and followed her. We walked out of the doors and I turned left to go through the doors into the ICU, but the nurse turned in the opposite direction.

"Where are we going?" I asked.

She opened a door on the left side to a small room and stood to the side to let me in, then closed the door behind her.

She spoke softly, "Mr. Miller, my name is Amy and I've been taking care of your wife tonight. I need to let you know that we've brought her out of sedation."

"Oh, thank God, that's great news."

"Mr. Miller, she's no longer intubated. We're giving her a generous dose of morphine for comfort."

Her expression didn't match the amazing news that she was telling me.

"I don't understand. You don't seem happy about it."

"Please have a seat."

I did as she said, and she began, "Toby, a couple of hours ago, Annaliese began showing signs of the Uncal type of a brain herniation."

"What the fuck does that mean?"

"There's excessive swelling in the innermost part of her brain, caused by the hematoma."

I'm sure I gave her a look that matched my comprehension of her words when I said, "You're not helping,"

"Mr. Miller, when she was brought in, there was blood pooling between her brain and her skull. The pooling caused pressure on the central part of her brain. When that happens, there's significant damage to the brain tissue deep on the inside."

"So, do the surgery where part of her skull is removed, man. Release the pressure, right?"

"Sir, that's only an option if the herniation is near the skull."

"What are you saying?"

"With the combination of the herniation visible by, what we call abnormal posturing—"

She took a deep breath

"So, why was she taken off of all of the machines?"

"Because the machines are a futile effort at this point. We want to give you the opportunity to see her before she goes, without all of the machines."

"Goes?"

I stared at her hoping she would tell me that Anna was about to be transferred somewhere. Maybe to another wing of the hospital, but I knew in my gut, that's not what she meant. I shook and yelled, "No! Oh, God, please no."

She gave me time to get my composure and I finally spoke, "How much time do I have?"

"Hours at the most."

I tried so hard to get control of my emotions, knowing I couldn't go back and see her like that but my emotions controlled me for the next ten minutes. *Hours,* I thought to myself and began to take deep breaths in through my nose and exhaled slowly out of my mouth until my shoulders stopped shaking and my breathing regulated.

"I think I'm ready," I told Amy.

"Mr. Miller, let me explain posturing before we go back there. Abnormal Posturing is an involuntary muscle reaction that makes the patient flex their arms and legs. In her case, her head is stretched back, looking upwards, her arms are extended by her sides with her wrists bent and her hands pointing down. Her legs are extended and her feet are pointing towards the curtain."

"Oh my God, is she in pain?"

"No, she's still in a coma. The morphine is keeping her very comfortable. The posturing will sometimes come and go, and without sedation, she may wake up slightly, but, it's likely she wouldn't be able to speak."

"I understand," I said.

"Sir, one more thing; even if she does start to wake and, by some miracle, is able to speak, she may not know who you are."

I could hardly comprehend the severity of what I had just heard. *How can this be it?* That's the only thought I had, and it repeated over and over like an unsynchronized, chanting mob.

Where was that confidence now? Where was the strength?

I took several deep breaths and tried my best to put on that façade I promised myself the night before. I looked up at her sympathetic eyes, swallowed hard and said with a manufactured smile, "That's okay, Amy," I reached my hand up to meet hers. "I still know who she is."

She placed her hand on the outside of my arm when I stood up to be sure I kept my balance.

"I'm so sorry, Mr. Miller. This is not how I saw this playing out."

I shook my head with a sarcastic laugh and replied, "Yeah, me neither."

We walked out of the small room and turned right, passed the waiting room and she entered the code into the panel by the doors to ICU. When we reached her room, the curtain was already pulled open. My overwhelming thought was how good it was to see her without the tube coming out of her mouth. The left side of her head was wrapped in gauze. Her lips were dry. As Amy described, her head was pointing upwards, and her arms and legs were stretched as far as her bones would allow. Her hands were pointing downwards and her feet pointed towards the curtain.

I glanced up at the brain activity monitor. The progressive wavy line that I saw a few hours before was barely moving, like a peaceful lake on a breezy day. Even with her blackened eyes, gauze around her head, the cast on her left arm, and her outstretched arms and legs, she somehow looked peaceful. I couldn't help but to think of the inevitable moment that I was facing within the next few hours. I turned to Amy, who was still standing at the entrance to the room.

"Amy, what can I expect when—when it's time?"

"Her brain will stop functioning, which will cause all of her organs to shut down, and her body will relax."

"Then what?" I asked.

"Nothing," she told me softly. "Because of the DNR order, there's nothing more we can do."

"What have I done?" I said, staring at her, hoping for some type of affirmation.

Amy stepped closer to me and said, "You've done the right thing, that's what you've done. Without that order, we would have to keep her intubated and add more machines. When the brain dies, we can keep the heart pumping, we can keep the lungs breathing. When we turn to life-saving techniques like that, technically she is alive, but the brain is still dead."

I sighed and turned back to Anna.

Amy closed the curtain part-way. "I'll leave you alone," she said, then closed it entirely.

Alone. The only thing in life that I'm afraid of is being alone. Alone with my thoughts, alone with my hobbies. No one to share my day with; my good times and bad. How insignificant a life can be when you're alone.

I walked next to her bed and took her hand with glassy eyes.

Her body relaxed. The black began to fade from her eyes, the gauze slowly disappeared. The cast fell away. Her eyes opened, and she turned to me with the most beautiful blue eyes I had ever seen. She was radiant. A smile stretched across her lips.

"Baby, why are you sad?" she said.

"Oh, Sweetheart, they tell me that—" I looked away.

"It doesn't matter, Toby. Nothing they say matters. Nothing that happens to me matters. What matters, honey, is that I know you love me. I've felt it every day since the day we met. And that's enough for me."

"I love you too, Annaliese, so, so much."

She shook my hand back and forth and whispered, "Hey."

I looked into her eyes again.

"Till death do us part, remember?" she said.

"I know, baby, I just—I thought we had more time. I'm sorry for all of the trivial bullshit. I'm sorry I worked overtime instead of spending the time with you. I'm sorry I ever disrespected you in any way. I'm sorry I spent so much time on my computer or playing the drums or playing games. I'm sorry—"

"Toby."

I stopped talking to look at her.

"I'm not. I'm not sorry for any of it. You lived your life, and that's the way it's supposed to be," she said.

"But, honey, I—"

"Shut up," she laughed and pulled my hand to her lips. "There's not much time and I don't want what's left to be filled with regrets. I have no regrets. I love you so much."

I smiled at her, "I love you too, Anna."

"You have to promise me a few things," she began. "First of all, keep living your life. You must live while you're still alive. Follow your dreams. Get that forever house in the mountains, follow your passion of landscape photography, keep writing, go on an Alaskan cruise, shoot waterfalls in Iceland. You do these things and I will always be with you. Baby, you have to promise me something else too."

"Anything, honey. Anything at all."

"I want you to keep chasing ghosts, but please don't look for me. I'm afraid it will only hurt both of us that much more. You have a gift. I need all of the equipment and you can just see them sometimes. I never understood that," she said with a laugh. "Keep the TV off. There's far too much hate in the world to waste the time you have left being

entertained by it. It will only make you angry and it's not worth it."

"I promise," I said. "I promise all of these things to you. I will miss you so much, Annaliese. You are my rock; my safe place. You've loved me, you've supported me and you've challenged me to be the best version of me that I can be."

Her smile faded, and she closed her eyes.

"Anna? Anna. Baby, please."

She turned to me again and said, "There's not much time, my love. You must live while you're alive. You are my everything and I will always love you. Kiss me one more time, Toby, please"

My eyes glossed over with tears. I leaned over and touched my lips to hers ever so gently on the corner of her mouth. I placed her hand back at her side and watched her as she closed her eyes again. Her arms and legs stiffened, and her head arched backwards. The bandages and cast returned, just like her blackened eyes.

The brain wave monitor became more active. The beeps became more frequent. The tension in her body faded as I held her hand. I felt my own hand being squeezed steadily, and I looked at her face. Her lips parted, and I watched them slowly form the words, "I love you."

Her hand went limp and the monitors were flat. Alarms sounded from the machines and a light flashed in the hallway. I pulled her hand to my lips and said, "I love you too, Anna. I always will."

Several nurses came into the room, including Amy. My knees weakened, and I was supported by Amy on my left and a male nurse on my right as they guided me out of the room. I turned to look one last time as they closed the curtain behind them. Before it closed completely, I saw, just for a second, a man. He was wearing a dark winter coat and was wearing a baseball cap, crying at the head of Anna's bed.

The next several hours of my memory were, and still are, as shattered as my heart. There are pieces all over the hospital that hold images of rooms I can't recall, people I've never met and sounds that have completely faded. Of the five senses, only one was prominent, an overwhelming feeling of emptiness.

My first vivid memory is when I was sitting in a small room and someone brought a blue folder and a large, white plastic drawstring bag to me, put their hand on my shoulder and respectfully said, "I think that's it, Mr. Miller."

I had been dismissed. That was it. There was nothing more for me at that hospital. I went into that place only twelve hours before carrying the heaviest load I had ever carried up to that point; fear, anxiety, confusion and hope, yes, hope. With the sun shining brightly, reflecting off the blanket of snow, my backpack was slung over my left shoulder, a large plastic drawstring bag nearly dragging on the floor by my feet and all I could think was that the weight of the load I was carrying out was a thousand times heavier than the one I walked in with. Not on my shoulder or in my hands, but in my heart.

The walk out to my truck felt like the longest I had ever taken. I threw my backpack, the folder and the drawstring bag in my back seat and closed the door. I turned around to look at the emergency room entrance with my mind as empty as my chest. I felt the cool air on my face and closed my eyes for a moment. I swayed from left to right with the breeze, took a deep breath and got in the truck. I slowly drove along the winding roads to exit the hospital grounds and took a right onto 82nd Street. As I approached Sargent Road, the light turned yellow, then red. I stared at the broken guard rail until I heard a horn from behind me. I looked up and inched forward through the already green light.

When I arrived home, I pulled into the garage and pushed the button to close the door before ever getting out of the vehicle. I don't know how long I sat there, numb, before getting out and gathering my backpack and the plastic drawstring bag and walked into the house through the garage entrance. I reached the end of the hallway, went straight across into the kitchen and set both bags down on the floor by the corner cabinet. I looked out of the kitchen into the living room through the cutouts in the walls. I looked around, moving only my eyes at the fireplace, the mantle, the candles, the cabinets, then the coffee table with the fondue pot and wilted fruit tray.

I made a promise to Anna that I would live my life. But how? How could I go on? How could I wake up in the morning, mow the lawn, buy groceries, cook meals, go out to eat, hang out with friends, watch movies and sleep at night? How could I ever live my life? Alone.

Chapter 4

A Promise Kept

I tried to keep myself busy, so I started by clearing off the coffee table. I put the fruit in the garbage disposal and the fondue pot on the counter, without a clue of how to get the hardened chocolate out of the pot. The house was already clean from the night before, so cleaning again wouldn't do any good. There were a few movies on the cabinet to the right of the fireplace, so I opened the player, put the movies in their cases and returned them to their spaces in alphabetical order in the enclosed shelves on the ends of the cabinets. An hour passed, just putting the movies away because I kept staring at— nothing. I just watched the ghosts of the past in different places throughout the house replaying memories of once upon a time.

I couldn't do any more. I just sat on the couch thinking. Thinking of the future, thinking of the past, thinking of what was, and what could never be. I got up a few times only to go to the bathroom and return to the couch. When nighttime fell, I got up from the couch and, for the first time, walked towards our room. I leaned with my right shoulder on the door frame and stared at the taught bed with several pillows and the black chemise I had laid out for her the night before. I never knew a person could cry so much.

I removed the decorative pillows and threw them in the closet, then carefully placed the chemise in her top drawer. I undressed completely, pulled the covers back and laid in the bed. With my eyes closed, I laid towards the middle of the mattress on my right side, facing the outside of the bed with a second pillow at the edge. I sensed the sweet smell of her perfume and I opened my eyes.

Anna stared back at me with a smile, with her head laying on praying hands placed gently on top of the extra pillow. It was so real, I could feel her laying against me. I reached out to touch her, but only felt the softness of the pillow as she slowly disappeared.

I smiled at the memory, then threw the pillow off the bed. I straightened my legs, tucked them up to my chest, rolled onto my back, then back to my right side again. I tried everything I could to empty my mind but nothing was working.

"Toby," I heard her whisper from behind me.

I rolled over onto my left side. There she was again with those piercing blue eyes and that perfect smile.

I tried something different that time. I figured that was only the first of many nights that I would lay down and see her smiling at me. A smile that seemed as though I had only seen it a few times, so I let her in. After all, that's not so bad, is it? With my eyes still open, I pulled her pillow from the top of the bed, pulled it close to me and threw my leg over it. I tucked my left arm underneath and wrapped my right around it tightly.

My cell phone launched into "New York State of Mind," from

Billy Joel; Anna's favorite. It was Monday morning and time to get up for work. I opened my eyes and turned off the alarm, stretched and looked over at Anna's pillow. It was empty.

I picked up my phone to call my boss, but just stared at it. Recognizing that I couldn't replay the events of the last thirty-six hours, I sent a text instead.

> Hey boss. I can't call or talk about it right now but I'll need some time off. Anna was in a car accident Saturday night. She didn't make it.

I watched the dots at the bottom of the screen flash, then disappear, then flash again and disappear again. A moment later, they flashed again, then disappeared. He finally sent a reply.

> Oh, God, Toby. I just don't know what to say to that. I am so sorry.

The dots flashed again.

> Take what you need, man. Keep me informed as you can.

I set my phone down and, a minute later, it vibrated. It was another text from my boss.

> How can I help? What can I do, man? If there's anything at all, you just let me know.

I looked over at the bed where my wife should have been and said, "Good morning, Sweetheart," as tears welled up in my eyes again.

She's gone. She's really gone.

I got out of bed, went to the closet and put my robe on before making a pot of coffee.

Now what? I need to call for services. What kind of service should I have for her? Where's her car? I need to contact the insurance company. I need to call her boss.

I tried to think of everything I needed to do as well as anything I *could* to keep myself busy. I thought of the blue folder and went to the garage to get it from the back seat and returned to the kitchen. There was information about funeral homes, pamphlets for survivors and a sheet with a phone number for a suicide hotline.

I poured myself a cup of coffee and called Anna's office and broke the news to her boss. She had worked as a manager at the same company for twenty-one years. We cried together. She offered any type of assistance I might need and requested I let her know when services were going to be.

From the blue folder, I looked over the list of funeral homes in the area. I called the only one that I recognized. It was the same one that Dad chose when we lost Mom six years before and that I chose when Dad died six months later. I set an appointment for that afternoon at 2:00. I'm not sure how I kept my composure throughout the appointment when my answers to some of their questions would ultimately become my wife's obituary.

The service was scheduled for Thursday afternoon at the church across the street. They told me I could put together photo albums and bring things to remember her by that they would place on a table in the back of the church.   With sympathetic handshakes, I left the funeral home.

I stopped at a drive-through on the way home and realized it was the first time I had eaten since Saturday night. I got home, ate my lunch, got my computer out of my backpack and sat on the couch to update the journal.

When I finished, I closed the computer and was surrounded by darkness. I didn't realize that I had been sitting there so long that the sun had set. I reached for the light on the end table next to me and turned it on when I found the knob and looked around the house again.

Just like the night before, loneliness washed over me. The silence in the house was anything but silent. My thoughts raced through my mind, echoing over the low buzz of the refrigerator. The morning wasn't as bad as I expected it to be. My thoughts were occupied in the afternoon at the funeral home, making it a little easier, but sitting there in that empty house at the time of day when I spent most of it with Anna; that was the worst.

For the next few weeks, that's how every day played out. The activities in the middle of the day changed, of course, but waking up in the mornings and going to bed at night were the same.

I saw Anna everywhere. I chose to focus my mind on the good times and to count it as a blessing that I saw her so much instead of missing her physical presence.

Sympathy cards piled up on the counter, the phone rang repeatedly but I rarely answered it. Although I was a terrible host, our friends still came to check on me. The day of her memorial, we celebrated her life during a small ceremony at the church where the funeral crashers outnumbered our friends and family. I was selfish that day. I didn't really offer consolation to anyone because I couldn't get beyond my own grief. Hell, I don't even really know who showed up.

For days, I either sat around the house in different chairs, drank, cried, screamed, or slept wherever I passed out; sometimes on the couch, sometimes in our bed.

The police gave me permission to search her car and retrieve anything I needed but I couldn't bring myself to do it. At some point, I received a check from the insurance company for the value of the car.

During those few weeks, I think I leaned on every wall of the house watching the version of Anna that my mind created, dancing foolishly through the living room, cooking, laughing, drying her hair, reading books, and playing games on her laptop. I imagined her doing all kinds of mundane tasks that meant nothing at the time but mean the world to me now.

In late April, I went to the mailbox, sifted through the letters and threw them on the counter with the rest, like I did most days. That's when the return address on one envelope caught my eye. I lifted the corner of the flap and opened the envelope on the short side and pulled out the check. I covered my mouth, conflicted from trying to decide on an appropriate emotion.

"Always taking care of me, aren't you, Sweetheart?" I said.

I shook my head in disbelief and offered a hint of a smile through more tears. The check from the life insurance company was written for an amount that I just couldn't wrap my head around. There was enough to pay off all of our debt, both vehicles, the house and still have enough left over to put in the savings account to live off of for at least a year. A thought entered my mind like an intruder stepping through a stranger's doorway - *The Forever House*. I heard Anna's voice as clearly as if she were standing right next to me.

Follow your passion of landscape photography, keep writing, go on an Alaskan cruise, shoot waterfalls in Iceland. You do these things and I will always be with you.

I looked around the house, focused on the framed prints of our photographs of waterfalls and other beautiful scenery from Tennessee. The first one I looked at was one of us in front of a cascade. I recalled when it was taken. It was sunny, and we had been married for less than forty-eight hours and one day after I had taken my first photograph on a manual setting of a point-and-shoot camera. We were in the Chimney Tops Picnic Area on the road towards Newfound Gap. I set the camera on the tripod and looked up and down the cascades for the perfect spot. Anna was my model as I took a few photos before setting the ten-second timer. I pushed the button and ran out to sit next to her on the large rock. I leaned down and placed my forehead against hers, then kissed her. We stood up and two elderly ladies sitting at a picnic table smiled at us grandly and asked how long we had been married. They wished us luck when I answered, and we were on our way.

The next one I focused on was us standing in front of Ramsey Cascade two years later. After hiking four miles and gaining 2,100 feet in elevation, the photograph reflected the first time we had smiled in at least two and a half miles. We didn't get back to our cabin until after dark. That was the same night that I locked the keys in the car and set off the alarm trying to open the door. As funny as it is to think about now, it certainly wasn't funny when it happened. People from all over the country were enjoying a romantic evening in a cabin high up on a Tennessee mountain, and my car alarm went off for fifteen minutes.

The next photo I looked at was not of the two of us, but of new growth at the base of the trees that were burned and blackened from the late November fire in 2016. We had visited in July of the following year and the undergrowth wasn't as prominent, but when that picture was taken three months later, there was life amid the death; and a hope that one day the vegetation would be thicker than ever before and that life in that place would go on regardless of how much had been burned.

I continued to look at the serene photographs of waterfalls, cascades, autumn scenes with auburn, yellow and red foliage and others that were close-ups of the flowers in the Springtime. We had vacationed there two or three times a year for the past ten years.

You have to live while you're still alive.

"I promise, my love. I promise" I said out loud.

I walked up to one winter scene. We were standing on a footbridge near the entrance to the National Park and she had her head against my chest; both of us looking into the camera.

The picture came to life and we smiled into each

*other's eyes, she leaned up and kissed me and it froze
again when we returned to the pose in the photo.*

I reached up and touched the photograph gently.

"It's time to go home, baby."

Chapter 5

She's Everywhere

I called the same realtor that sold us the house twelve years before who advertises as, "Your realtor for life." He told me to do what I needed to, and that once the house was empty, he would take care of everything.

Packing up the house was every bit as emotional as I expected it would be. I went through every cabinet, closet, and drawer, simplifying what I could. Determining what to do with her personal things was much more difficult than I thought it would be. In the end, I did what I thought Anna would want; I gathered her clothes in plastic trash bags and donated all of it; all except her wedding gown. It was hard to get rid of it all, but not as hard as seeing it day after day.

The next morning when I woke up, I greeted Anna with a smile like I did every day and went to the kitchen to make a cup of coffee from a single serve pod. When it finished brewing, I gathered enough clothes for a few days, put them in a small suitcase and loaded it into the Sorento along with my camera equipment and a small cooler of drinks. After a shower and shaving my beard that had been growing for weeks, I filled up my gas tank and got on the interstate.

I rolled Anna's window down when I drove over the Ohio River, like she did every time we drove over the bridge on I-275. I laughed out loud as I approached the Tennessee state line. Anna always tried to take a picture of the huge blue sign. Being around a line of trees, she always got a blurry picture. I took the Gatlinburg exit off of I-40 and continued past Sevierville. The sky was clear and it seemed like I could see forever. When I broke up over the hill and the majestic view of Mount LeConte came into sight, it was breathtaking. As many times as we had been there, I've always gotten excited when that mountain comes into view. This time, without Anna, I simply smiled.

I pulled into the hotel around 4:00 and put my suitcase in my room. I had to bite my lip to hold back tears. Every time we didn't get a cabin in the woods or on the mountain, Anna and I stayed there. I pulled a business card out of my wallet for the owners of the last cabin we stayed in back in October. It was a small cabin on a secluded piece of property, with a hot tub on the large wooden deck out the back door.

On that trip, we arrived at the cabin around 2:00 in the morning with a code to unlock the door, but the code didn't work. We drove back into town and checked several hotels, and none had any rooms available. Finally, at 3:15 a.m., we found a hotel with just one room. I told the man at the front desk, "That's great. I only need one room."

When we got settled for the night, we emailed the owners to let them know about the code for the front door. After four hours of sleep, Anna checked her phone and already had a response with a sincere apology for the error and that they were on their way to the cabin immediately to correct the situation.

We didn't leave the hotel for another hour and stopped to get breakfast to make sure they had an opportunity to fix the door before we arrived. After breakfast, we drove out to the cabin and were surprised that they were still there and were just finishing up. We had never met the owners of a cabin we stayed in, so it was a great experience. They explained that they were from Ohio and owned three cabins in the area. We talked to them for at least an hour and they invited us to their house about twenty minutes away from there at some point during our stay. While we talked, they shared their story of how amazing their realtor was and when it was time for us to get our forever house, to let them know and they would connect us.

There I was sitting in a hotel room in Gatlinburg, Tennessee dialing the number for our new friends to have them connect me to their amazing realtor.

Linda answered the phone and I reintroduced myself. To my surprise, she immediately apologized again for the problem with the door code in October and asked what she could do for me.

"Linda," I started. "Annaliese was in a car accident about 6 weeks ago."

"Oh, Toby, I'm so sorry. Is she okay?"

I paused before saying, "She didn't make it, Linda."

"Oh, God Toby, I'm sorry to hear that. That's awful. How are you holding out?"

"Some days aren't as bad as others. It's really all about learning to live a different way. Trying to live without her with me. I imagine being here will not be easy, but she made me promise that I'd keep living and follow our dream of moving here, like we talked about back in October."

"Is that why you came?" she asked.

"Yes," I said with a smile. "I remember you telling me about how much you liked your realtor."

"Alex? Oh, I could talk about her forever. There's nobody better in the business. Do you want me to call her?"

"Yes, ma'am, I'd appreciate that."

"Ok, I'll call her right away."

"Oh, it doesn't have to be this afternoon. Just whenever you get a chance."

"Toby, I won't have it any other way. I insist. Is this your cell phone that you called from?"

"Yes."

"I'll let you know when I've gotten a hold of her. Are you okay if I give her this number?"

"Of course. Thank you."

I looked around the room when I hung up the phone, walked out to the balcony overlooking LeConte Creek and leaned on the railing. The sun was setting to my right. A car occasionally drove past on the road across the creek. People were bustling around on the sidewalks below. Couples were holding hands, groups of friends were laughing. I watched them and thought to myself how life goes on, even after I lost my beloved Anna. The Earth kept turning and the people below weren't sharing my grief.

Maybe this is what Anna meant when she told me to live my life.

My phone vibrated in the case attached to my belt clip.

"Hello."

"Hi Toby, it's Alex with—"

"Oh, hi Alex.   How are you?"   I interrupted while secretly admiring her amazing Tennessee accent.

"Linda tells me that you're looking for a place."

"Yes, I am."

"I have several properties that I can show you depending on what you're looking for. Do you have plans for early morning?"

"No, ma'am, I don't."

"I'll come pick you up at 8:00, is that okay? It's supposed to be really nice tomorrow; first day of May," she said excitedly.

"Yes, it is," I confirmed

"I got so sick of the cold this year. It normally doesn't bother me, but this year was awful," she said.

"It was up North, too.   I heard the cold blast reached this far South. You're not used to that kind of cold, are you?"

"Hell no, we're not. Maybe in the upper elevations with a wind, but not down here in town."

I laughed at her casual style and she continued with, "We'll find a nice picnic table in the park and you can tell me about your dream home."

"Wow, that's fast. I certainly didn't expect—"

"Nonsense! Any friend of Doug and Linda's is a friend of mine."

"I really appreciate that, Alex."

"Oh, it's just a whole lot of nothin', sweetie. I'll see you in the morning."

I went back inside the room and sat in the desk chair, pivoting back and forth. I considered how hard it was going to be to walk the streets of Gatlinburg and to drive around the park. I had never been there without Anna.

> *I felt a hand on my shoulder and a whisper in my ear, "Let's go for a walk."*
>
> *I reached my own hand up to touch hers, turned around and looked up to kiss her.*
>
> *"That's perfect. Let's go."*

I made sure I had my room key when I walked out the door to join the crowds of people on the sidewalk. There was loud music playing that faded from one attraction to another as I walked. Every other block, someone was handing out coupons for their own attraction somewhere else along the strip. The smell of different foods wafted through the town. Several musicians were out on the streets that evening with guitar cases open as they played popular mountain favorites.

One gentleman caught my attention the second he started singing. He had a soulful sound with a deep voice and sang slowly, and deeply. I knew right away that he wasn't just singing, he was bestowing upon all who could hear him the ability to truly feel the notes in his voice. He shared the age-old story of the two strangers that climbed 'ol Rockytop looking for a whiskey still. His melody seemed to silence all other sounds until his voice was reverberating beautifully. People stopped to listen. Others even crossed the street to hear him closer. When he sang the very last words, his voice sustained the note for several seconds as it faded. The crowd burst with applauds and threw money in his guitar case just as I did.

I crossed the street to start back towards the hotel. It was an incredibly pleasant walk—until I reached the intersection at Stoplight 8. I looked up the street and, in the distance, saw the entrance to the park and the access to the Motor Nature Trail, a driving trail Anna and I frequented. Sometimes three, four; even five times a day. Some of our greatest photographs came from there. It was typically the first and last thing we did during our vacations. Time seemed to have frozen as I stood there staring along the road.

I felt someone bump into me and scolded, "Dude, what are you doing?" I looked around and there was a crowd of people ebbing along the crosswalk while I was, once again, mesmerized by memories of my past.

"Sorry, man!" I said when I started moving with the crowd again.

I returned to the hotel and carried the cooler to the vending area to add more ice and went back to the room. I went to the balcony again, but not without an ice-cold beer this time.

Alex will be here in the morning asking about The Forever House. She wants to know about the 'dream home.' Strange; I hadn't thought about it that much. I guess I didn't want to formulate some perceived version of perfection and be disappointed. I sure wish Anna was here right now. Wonder what it will be like to live on my own. The house! Damn! What is my dream home?

The combination of the seven-hour drive and the beer had me nodding in the chair on the balcony while I tried to formulate a vision of my dream home; the perfect place—The Forever House.

"Goodnight, my love."

My alarm woke me in the morning in enough time to get breakfast at the hotel, taste their amazing coffee and get ready for the day with Alex. From the time I woke up, I thought about the dream home. After a shower and another clean shave, I waited at the entrance under the hotel awning for her.

At 7:59, a car pulled in, turned around in the narrow parking lot and stopped right in front of me. She got out of the car quickly and started walking towards me. She was an attractive woman, not much shorter than me with medium length brunette hair and confidence that stretched for two states. She dressed modestly; not overly professional like many realtors do.

"Toby."

I smiled and started walking towards her with an outstretched hand.

"I'm Alex, it's really good to meet you," she confirmed while shaking my hand before her tone changed and I knew that Linda must have told her about Anna. "I've heard a little about why you're here beyond buying your dream home."

I matched her tone and shook my head, "Yes."

She smiled with sad eyes, then, excitedly said, "So, are you ready to go?"

I smiled back, "I sure am."

I was surprised, and equally as grateful at the fact that she didn't ask any further questions. She just let it go. Up to that point, everyone wanted to sympathize with me when they didn't really know anything about Anna. Alex was different; at least she seemed to be.

She opened her door and got into the car while I stood there, not really knowing what to do or how to act. She partially stepped back out and looked over at me, "Well, get on in. There's no one down here gonna open your door for you."

I was still laughing lightly when I stepped into the car. She threw her hair to her left side to look at me and said, "What?"

I opened my eyes wide with a smile and said, "Nothing."

She put the car into gear and turned right out of the parking lot.

"You know what I think?" she asked, smiling the whole time. "I think that 'nothing' is almost always 'something,' so what's got you so tickled?"

I turned to her with a smirk and simply said, "Nothing."

She poked me on the arm and said, "We're going to have to work on our communication, Toby."

We were crossing over Ski Mountain Road where Gatlinburg ends, and the National Park begins; still showing signs of the fire. I stared out the window for what seemed like hours and Alex spoke softly.

"Hey—you okay?"

"Anna and I took our picture on that footbridge right there. It was February, with a light snow." I paused for a moment as we got a little farther. "We also walked that trail right over there several times through the years." I pointed to the trail where someone was jogging.

I kept looking out the window as we passed by the visitor's center that we had gone into at least 30 times.

"She's everywhere, Alex," I muttered.

"I know, Sweetie, I know," she said as she touched my hand lightly. "We're almost at the Chimney Tops Picnic Area. It's just up here on the right."

I looked at Alex just as my lip tightened and I lost control of a single tear that fell out of the corner of my left eye.

"I know."

Chapter 6

The Forever House

We pulled into the Chimney Tops Picnic Area and parked near the creek. Alex had a cooler in her back seat and offered me a bottle of water before we sat on the picnic bench.

"So," she began. "Tell me about your dream house."

"Anna called it our Forever House."

"Ok, then, Forever House it is. Tell me all about it. We'll work out the details later, but for now, I just want to hear about your perfect Forever House."

"Every time we talked about it, I imagined a large piece of property; like 4 acres or more. The area with the house will be clear enough to have a lush green lawn to tend to where all the mature trees are far enough away that, if they fall, they wouldn't damage the house. I want a creek to flow through the property, so I can take a cheap-ass lawn chair and sit in it with my feet in the water. I'm a photographer, so the creek will be lined on both sides with rhododendron but have enough of an opening to access both the creek and the rest of the property. It needs to be secluded. I want to sit outside and hear nature, not road noise."

Alex feverishly wrote down every detail that I explained. I turned my eyes to the water cascading over the huge rocks and let my imagination take over.

"I want a stone patio with part of it enclosed as a four-season room and the rest of it open-faced, but still covered. The open part would have a fire pit and the enclosed part, a fireplace with a rocking chair. I want a covered front porch. I want French doors from the master bedroom that lead to a hot tub that can also be accessed from outside. I want a breakfast nook that faces East with floor to ceiling windows. I want more light on the North side of the house than on the South so that it doesn't get so damn hot with the afternoon sun."

I interrupted the tour that was playing out in my mind to clarify, "Not that I don't want any windows facing South, I just—"

Alex had stopped writing and looked at me without expression.

"What is it?" I asked.

She spoke softly, "Nothing." She forced a tiny smile that only lifted the corner of her mouth. "Keep going."

"Now, Alex, somebody once told me that 'nothing' is almost always 'something,' so what did I say?"

"Really—it's nothing."

She sighed, smiled bigger and said, "Really, Toby, it's nothing. Keep going. You're doing great."

"I want a detached outbuilding that I could use for storage and a woodshop."

She threw her pen down on the picnic table and said intently, "Where did you come from?"

The question wasn't as surprising as the look she gave me. She seemed to look right through me.

"What do you mean?" I asked.

"I think I've heard enough. Before you explain any more, I have a place I think you'll like."

"Really? Is it similar to what I'm explaining at all?"

She laughed as she put her elbows on the table, folded her hand together and leaned toward me with an expression I couldn't read.

"Toby," she started and looked down at the table. "You're explaining a property that's been on the market for almost a year now. It's well kept, and the house has been maintained. Can I show you?"

"Well, of course, let's check it out?"

She looked up at me again and smiled, "Let's check it out," she repeated without looking at me.

We got into the car and left the picnic area. Somewhere on the other side of Gatlinburg, she turned off the main road to an area I had never been to before. It was a windy, hilly road. She turned on her left turn signal, but I couldn't see a break in the trees until we actually turned onto a roughly paved, one-lane road. We had to have driven another half a mile with no other houses or cabins before we turned off the road again to the right onto a long, rock driveway. We broke through the trees to an opening in the woods and faced a beautiful home with a wrap-around wooden porch surrounded by thick, green grass. There was another building that sat behind the house and off to the right, just at the edge of the woods that looked like a three-car garage.

"Okay, this is a little creepy." I said.

"Creepy? In what way?" she asked.

"Not, like, scary creepy, but it's so much like what I've imagined all these years."

"Wait until you see inside," she said.

We walked up three steps onto the porch and she entered a code into the realtor lock on the front door, got the key out and opened the front door.

A feeling of peace washed over me. The kitchen was to the left with a curved bar countertop separating the kitchen from the dining room. I turned to my immediate right to see another stone wall separating a galley style kitchen and the living room. There were two arched cutouts with a range and oven in one and an indoor grill in the other. Alex stepped to the side into the kitchen looking into the lower row of cabinets and I walked past the stone wall into the living room. The other side of the stone wall had a fireplace. The dining room was open to the living room and on the wall opposite from the front door was a sliding door that accessed a covered wooden balcony. I stepped out and immediately to my left was another door to access an all-season room with another small fireplace. Beyond the fireplace was a large, six-person hot tub.

I turned around to look at Alex, who was standing just outside the sliding door with a smile. I shook my head slowly at the similarity to my description but didn't say a word.

"Didn't I tell you?" she said.

I remained silent when I turned back around, facing the hot tub and noticed another sliding door. I tried to open the door, but it was locked.

"Oh, sorry about that," Alex stated. "I'll go unlock it from the inside."

I looked around while I waited for her and she slid the blinds open on the inside. I heard the click of the lock and a whoosh from the door sliding open. I stepped up into the Master bedroom. There was a raised floor on the right wall with a half-circle stained glass window at eye level; a perfect spot for a king-sized bed. There was a walk-in closet on each side of the raised floor and a door on the other side of the distant closet.

I stepped through the door into the master bathroom. Most of the walls were drywall, except the wall with a four by six stand-up shower with three shower heads; one on each wall and one hanging from the ceiling. That wall was made of stone, similar to the one separating the living room and the galley kitchen with an arched doorway and glass doors to enter the shower. To my right were double sinks, another stone wall and the toilet set to the side of the shower.

"This bathroom is amazing, Alex."

"Yes, it is."

I turned to go back into the bedroom and directly in front of me was a set of French doors that opened inwards to access the dining room with the kitchen to my right and the dining room immediately to my left. I walked through the living room and there were three doors, separated quite evenly to bedrooms on each end and a bathroom in the middle.

The bedrooms were not as elaborate as the Master Bedroom, but, although smaller, the bathroom was quite similar to the one I had just seen at the other end of the house. The only differences were that the second bathroom had a single sink and the stand-up shower was smaller with a single shower head.

"I'm just a bit stunned here," I said.

"This is the 'nothing' I mentioned earlier. You described it as though you've been here before."

I didn't respond. There was nothing to say.

"Ready to see downstairs?" she asked.

"Downstairs?"

"Yes."

I followed her through the galley kitchen. Just to the right of the bedroom door toward the front of the house was another door I hadn't seen. I followed her down the steps as we entered a finished basement. There was a tiny bar on one end and installed recliner theater seating on the other, facing a widescreen proportioned wall with a black frame around the edges and a bathroom in the middle. There was a row of blinds covering a sliding door in the middle of the back wall.

"What's that?" I asked.

Alex smiled and said, "Take a look," with a wave of her hand.

I walked through the door to the outside onto a concrete patio on the ground level looking out towards the woods behind the house, edged by an empty flower bed.

I looked over at the detached garage, about fifty yards at an angle to my right. I asked Alex, "Can we check out the garage?"

"Which one?" she asked.

I gave her a puzzled look and she said, "There's a tiny, one-car garage through that other door on the basement wall."

"I didn't even see a door there."

"That's because all you could see was the bar," she said with a laugh.

"If that's just a little one-car, will you show me that one?" and I pointed to the detached garage in front of us.

"Of course."

She unlocked and opened the door to reveal a wide-open, finished garage with a coated floor and cabinets on the back wall; perfect for the Sorento, another car, if I chose to get one, and yard equipment. Not to mention a woodshop in the back.

"Want to see the creek?" she asked.

"Are you fucking kidding me? Sorry, I just—"

"It's okay, I cuss like a sailor when no one's around. You won't offend me."

"I really don't think I need to see any more." I stated.

"Shall we go back upstairs?"

"Yeah, let's do that."

She locked all of the doors behind us as we passed through them to go back upstairs. We leaned on the granite bar top separating the kitchen and the dining room.

"I know it's early," she started. "but if you decide you want it, I'll need a preapproval letter."

"That's not going to be necessary."

She gave me a puzzled look.

I smiled and said, "First of all, yes, I want it. How much are we talking here?"

"Two hundred and thirty-five thousand."

"And, who do I make the check out to?"

She was surprised at my question and just looked at me. I sarcastically spoke slowly, "Who—do—I—make—the—check—out—to?"

"Uh, I guess, if you just write it out to me, I'll take care of it."

I turned my head and looked at her out of the corner of my eye, "Can I trust you that much?"

Her expression was intent, and she said, "Toby, I will take care of it. You write the check and I'll remove the realtor locks and turn the keys over to you. You can stay here tonight if you want."

"Well, considering I have nothing to sit on or sleep on, I think I'll pass, but thank you."

I wrote the check for the amount she told me and looked around at my new house while she wrote down the address so that I could find it again. I got in the car and closed the door as Alex started the car. I looked over at her and said very sincerely, "Thank you."

"Oh, it's nothing."

"Nothing is always something, right? I mean it, Alex. Thank you. I really appreciate you taking the time with me today."

She gently placed her hand on top of mine that was resting on my thigh. I started to wrap my fingers around hers, but instantly realized that she wasn't Anna and it was not okay to hold my realtor's hand.

"You're welcome, Toby," she said as I pulled my hand away. I took a drink of water, so it wasn't so obvious that I had just jerked my hand away from hers.

"Is Toby your full name?"

"It's actually Tobias."

"Ooh, that's a manly name; strong."

"Let me guess, yours is actually Alexis."

"Alexandra." She made a face as though she was vomiting.

"You don't like it?" I asked.

"Hell no, Tobias. Alexandra is old-fashioned. Do I look old-fashioned to you?"

"No, ma'am," I said with a grin. "but I think Alexandra is a very pretty name."

She smiled and said, "Thank you," then changed the subject. "I would offer you lunch, but I do have a couple of appointments today. I assume you're okay to find a place to eat?"

"Of course."

We got back to the hotel shortly after noon and I went into my room, closed the curtain so that just a sliver of light was peeping through, undressed and laid in the bed.

"We did it, baby. We got The Forever House. I would do anything to have you back, to see you, to talk to you, to touch you one more time. If I had known the last time we went out to dinner would be our last, I would have opened every door. If I had known it was going to be the last time we talked, I would have told you I love you one more time. If I had known when you went out with the girls it would be the last, I would have held you tighter—and longer. This was supposed to be our big adventure; our end-game."

I listened to the buzz of the air conditioner turn on for a minute, then off again.

"I wish I had just one more, Anna. Just one more kiss. Just one more phone call. Just one more movie to watch. One more drink together. One more game night. Just one more bottle of wine. Just one more sunrise from the hot tub. One more cup of coffee. One more road trip. Just one more laugh—and one more cry. When it's the end, baby, I guess we always want what we can't have—just one more night."

Chapter 7

Shivers

I woke up and frantically looked around for the time. It was 7:38 p.m., but I was still tired. I got up to use the bathroom and stood in the middle of the room looking around in the darkness. The light peeking through the curtain was much dimmer. I crawled into bed and went back to sleep.

The next morning, I woke up a 5:45 starving and completely charged from all the sleep. I reached beside me for the switch on the nightstand light and turned it on. My eyes were wide and I shook my head to wake up even more. I stretched and shouted, "Goooooooood Morning." I rubbed my eyes and said, "Man, I've got a lot of shit to do."

I dressed in the same clothes I wore the day before, packed up the truck and was on the road by 6:20. My first stop was a drive-through breakfast. My list of things to do was getting bigger and consumed my thoughts.

With Anna's stuff gone, there's less to pack. I can probably get a rental and move it all myself, putting the Sorento on a trailer behind the rental truck. Hmm, the kitchen seems a little bit smaller, but that's okay, I don't have that much left since I simplified. Oh, there's the stone wall with the two cooktops. Are there cabinets over there? I don't remember. I wonder what Alex is doing right now.

I shook that last thought from my mind, then wondered why she entered so easily in the first place.

The living room only has the TV hanging on the wall, the two cabinets I built, the couch and the loveseat. Then the dining room with the four-top table and chairs. Should I keep the same bed? It will be a new place, so I think it will be okay. I've slept in it before, actually most nights now. Then the dresser, two end tables and the TV on the wall. Man, she looked good yesterday; and that accent— damn.

"Tobias Miller, Stop it!" I said out loud.

Live your life could mean many things, I guess. Let's see, what's upstairs? Oh boy, that's where all the shit is that we didn't know where to put anywhere else. I guess I can get rid of the treadmill. I'm sure as hell not going to use it. I'll take the exercise bike and the rowing machine; the two bookshelves, the TV, and the stand. There's a king-sized bed in one of the spare rooms, a dresser and—hmm, I guess that's it. The other room upstairs has my Mom's old desk that I built for her, another desk with a hutch, a filing cabinet, and my drum set. Then there's all the shit in the closets. Oh, and the attic above the garage.

My thoughts went to Alex several times on the way home. I tried to ignore them but couldn't. I thought about when she placed her hand on mine to comfort me and how I felt some strange connection to her that I couldn't explain. I did the best I could to dismiss all of the thoughts of Alex, but I couldn't eliminate them completely.

I stopped at a grocery store a half mile from my house to see if they had boxes they could give me to pack. The cashier told me to drive around back because they put all of their boxes back there. I was welcome to take as many as I wanted. When I pulled around the back of the store, a young kid with a bloody apron was standing by a back-door, smoking.

"Can I help you, sir?" he asked.

"I'm looking for boxes."

"We've got a bunch right over here, but they're all broken down already if that's okay."

"That's perfect."

"Any certain size you need?"

"I'm moving, so nothing too big; I wouldn't be able to carry it anyway."

He grabbed as many flattened boxes as he could between his hands and, with his cigarette hanging out of the corner of his mouth, said, "Open the hatch. I'll load them in for you."

"Thanks, man. I appreciate it."

He put in two more stacks of boxes and I closed the hatch and went home.

The house seemed different somehow. The best way I can explain it is that it felt less like home than it ever had. When I went inside, I looked around like I had so many times in the last six weeks. Instead of being so full of emotions and memories, it felt—empty.

I got a tape gun from upstairs and put boxes together one by one and started in the living room, packing up books, movies, and trinkets from the cabinets. When it was all empty, I moved upstairs. I kept taping and boxing, using the living room as a staging area. I put on loud music and kept packing until almost midnight when the only things left to pack were the kitchen and the master bedroom. I had no idea how long it would take to pack. My best guess was several days, but when I turned everything off and went to bed, I knew I could finish in a few more hours the next morning.

I laid down that night with my head turned to Anna's pillow, but it was empty. I reached my hand out and placed it on her pillow, rubbing it lightly; still nothing. The silence was deafening. All I could hear was a slight ringing in my ear from the music playing so loudly in the house for hours. I guess 80s Metal will do that to a guy.

I woke the next morning and called to rent the biggest truck possible with a car trailer, then called a couple of old friends to help me that afternoon. We laughed so hard our stomachs hurt like we used to years ago. It turned out to be a sort of balancing act in the huge truck to fit the last few pieces in, but we got it all in. It was almost nightfall when we finished, and a thought crossed my mind.

I had an expression of defeat when I said to my friends, "You are not going to believe this."

"Oh, shit, what?" one of them said.

Then the other spoke up, "Don't tell me you forgot something in the house, because if we open that door, I'm afraid shit's going to pop out of there like a Jack-in-the-box."

"Um—the bed is somewhere in the front half of the box truck." I stated.

They both broke out in hysterics, doubling over trying to catch their breath from laughing so hard at me.

"You can stay with us tonight, man. We've got an extra room if you want."

The other spoke up and said, "I'd offer too, but the kids are having a sleepover tonight."

We stood in the driveway, silent for a minute and I looked into the empty garage with a sigh, then looked back at my friends. One spoke up and said, "We're right behind you, man."

We walked inside, and I took one more look in every room, closet and drawer with my friends right with me. When we finished, I stood in the kitchen and looked out towards the living room. My memory flickered with visions of how it looked the night of Anna's accident. I took a deep breath and said, "I guess that's it."

We walked out to the garage and I said goodbye before following my pal over to his house for the night. I opened the door to the Sorento, reached up to the mirror and pushed the button to close the garage door. When the door met the concrete, it felt so final. I scanned the front of the house before starting the rental, releasing the parking brake and inching out to the street with the Sorento in tow. I watched the house grow distant in the mirrors as I passed into my purgatory of life. I was driving away from one life, but not yet towards a new one.

I woke up before sunrise the next morning, got dressed and crept downstairs towards the front door.

"Thought you were going to leave without saying goodbye?" I

heard my friend behind me.

"Yeah, I was hoping so."

"Not a chance, my friend."

I walked over and threw my arms around him.

"I'll be in touch, man, alright?" I said as we patted each other's backs the way men do before letting go.

"You better. I'll drive down there and find your ass if it's too long. We've been through too much to let go now."

"Dude, I was so fucked up, I don't even know if you were at the memorial service for her."

"I was right behind you the whole time, as always."

"I don't know why I don't remember that."

"Man, you had a lot to deal with."

"Yeah, I guess so," I said.

"I'm sure going to miss her," he told me.

"Yeah, man, me too. I better get on the road. This isn't going to be the normal seven-hour trip with that beast of a truck."

"Take it easy, man."

I smiled, remembering how we used to play this out as single guys before we both got married, "I'll take it any way I can get it."

"Hell, if you like it, take it again."

We laughed until we had to catch our breath.

"That will never get old."

"No, it won't."

I turned to him and said, "Tell your lovely wife I said hi and I'll see you two soon, I hope."

"Definitely."

I walked out his front door and didn't turn back, but I heard him close and lock the door behind me.

I got on the interstate just as the light was showing in the East. It was a quiet drive and I had to stop more than usual to get gas. My thoughts were mostly empty, but occasionally I thought of Anna, my friends I just left or how I was going to arrange everything in the new house. I stopped for gas just North of Knoxville for the last time on the trip. After filling my tank, I ordered some food from the restaurant inside.

While waiting for my number to be called, I pulled my phone out of its case and opened my contacts. The first one on the list was Alex. I smiled and hovered my finger over her number, then over the message icon and touched it. The blank screen came up with Alex's name at the top, and the keyboard at the bottom with the cursor in the message box. I looked at it for a moment, shook my head, then pushed the home button and put the phone back in the belt clip just as my order was ready.

I got back on the road, drove the rest of the way and pulled up to my new house early in the afternoon. I disconnected the Sorento from the truck and started taking things inside right away, starting with the perishables in the cooler and followed by the king-sized bed. I had to see what it looked like on the raised floor under the stained-glass window and the end tables on each side. I brought in the dresser, TV and my clothes to finish setting up the master bedroom.

Some of the furniture was slow to get into the house; carrying it a few feet at a time until I, at least, got it into its proper room or into the garage. The dolly and straps helped. I didn't stop until the back of the rental was empty and it was almost nightfall. I locked the vehicles, went inside and closed the door behind me.

"Please, let there be hot water."

I walked over to the kitchen sink and turned on the faucet, passing my fingers through the water quickly several times.

"Oh, thank God," I said as the water ran warm. I turned the water off again and scanned the mess in the house. "Big adventure, my ass."

I found the box with the bedsheets and made the bed before taking a shower. I had my travel hygiene kit and a towel readily available specifically for this moment. I adjusted the water temperature until it was perfect for me to step into, then stood in the middle of the arched shower with water coming at me from both sides and falling on me from above. It was, quite possibly, the best shower I had ever taken in my life. Steam was filling the bathroom. Even after getting clean, I stood with the water falling on me, occasionally pushing the water out of my eyes and turning the water hotter.

Oh, I have so much left to do. I just want to be done. Hope I packed my magic wand, so I can bippity boppity boo this shit into its place.

I turned my neck from side to side, letting the water heat my muscles as I stretched them. I bent down and stretched my legs and lower back, then reached to turn the water just a little hotter but the knob wouldn't turn anymore. I had maxed out the heat. The lights flickered, and I suddenly felt cold. It was a kind of cold that oozed from the inside making my entire body shiver; something I'd have to get used to in a new place that I wasn't yet familiar with.

I stood in the shower a little longer to make sure I was warm until the water temperature started to drop, and I knew I had used all the hot water from the tank. I shut the water off, stepped out to grab my towel, dried off and wrapped it around my waist. I turned on the light next to the bed and walked around the house turning the rest of the lights off and got between the sheets.

I looked around the amazing room with pride before reaching for the light to turn it off. The darkness was like nothing I've experienced since I was in the Army in New Mexico, listening to coyotes howling on a moonless night. My eyes were wide open, but I couldn't see my hand in front of my face, and all of my senses were piqued. Click—squeak—tick. I listened as the house seemed to come to life in the darkness.

Still wide-eyed, I turned the light back on and turned over on my side in hopes that I would sleep until sunrise.

Chapter 8
Connection

To my delight, the next thing I knew, I was waking up to a bright sunlit room. I went into my closet to get my robe, walked over to the vertical blinds and pushed them open, revealing the hot tub and the four-season room. I slid the glass door open and walked out. It was a beautiful day; peaceful. I opened the door to the covered porch and stepped out. It was perfect. The sun was above the horizon to my left. The dew on the grass glistened. There were birds chirping. One was standing on the electrical wires between the garage and the house throwing his head back and singing a distinct song. A rabbit ran across the yard from behind the garage. The tree line was about fifty yards in front of me with a view of the mountains over the tree line to the right and I could hear the faint flow of water. *Coffee*, I thought to myself. *Now if I could only find the coffee maker.* It was in the second box I looked in along with the coffee pods, sugar, and four mugs. I set it up on the bar counter against the wall and got the peppermint creamer out of the refrigerator. I walked through the house until I heard the last streaming flow of coffee trickle into my coffee cup.

Most of the furniture in the living room was in its place already, other than some minor adjustments for wall spacing. After opening the sliding glass door between the living room and the porch to get a cool breeze, I plugged in the speaker bar for the living room TV and placed it on the mantle. I was prepared so that, later in the day, if it got too quiet, I could fill the air with mood music; perhaps some Three Days Grace, Fallout Boy, or something classic like Alice Cooper, Judas Priest, Ozzy or Iron Maiden. Anna hated Iron Maiden, so I figured listening to them would give me the best chance of not reminiscing about her as much.

I spent the day setting up the spare bedroom in the room towards the back of the house, and my office in the bedroom towards the front, next to the entrance to the basement. The garage was big enough that I set up my woodworking tools in the back and placed everything else in a 'sufficient place that was good enough for that moment'. The last thing I did was carry some of the alcohol to the small bar in the basement and set up my electronic drum set next to it.

The house was certainly bigger than the last one, so some areas looked empty, like the entire front porch. I knew I would be shopping a lot over the next few days to fill some of the space. My immediate list included a riding mower, rocking chairs for the porches, a trailer for the Sorento, some sort of four-wheeler and groceries—Oh, and several night lights. I also called to get all of the utilities in my name and to get TV and Internet.

I started by hooking up my SUV to the back of the rental to return it then went to get an enclosed trailer and lawn mower, then stopped at the grocery store. I got into the long checkout line and pulled out my phone again, unlocked it and pulled up the messenger app. Alex's blank message from the restaurant the day before came up right away. I considered sending a message several times as I inched my cart forward when the line moved.

I typed, 'Hey there, Ale' and deleted it. 'Hi A' and deleted it again. 'Alex, it's Tob,' and again, deleted it. I finally pushed the home button and put my phone away.

When I got home, I put the groceries away first then unloaded the trailer, with the lawn mower still in it, into the garage. I locked everything up, went inside for a beer and pulled one of the dining room chairs out to the back porch.

Almost everything was unpacked except for the boxes, but I had had enough for that day. I looked around, and for the first time, really thought about the fact that everything I was looking at was mine. I listened to the creek somewhere back in the woods, the sun was close to the mountains in the distance. I wondered how far back the creek was and how much more of the property belonged to me.

Hmm, a reason to contact Alex.

I pulled my phone from my pocket again to start typing a message. When I pulled up her name, I contemplated if I should send something or not. That's when I saw three dots show up at the bottom, then disappear. *Holy shit, she's sending something to me*, I thought. I smiled and waited for her message, but never received one. I just watched as the dots appeared and disappeared four different times. When they stopped flashing, I put my phone back on my belt and sipped my beer.

What's left? The boxes. I should probably start with the kitchen. That's where most of the boxes belong anyway. Book ideas—what to write? Anna said I should try my hand at fiction after my first book. What are people reading these days? Romance, vampires, fantasy— maybe that's mostly for teens. Why fiction? What the hell do I write that hasn't already been written?

I kept scanning the property and thought of how much Anna would have loved this place. My thoughts suddenly went to the last night I talked to her.

Hope you're not too tired – It's Saturday. You're the most beautiful girl in the world and I want to spoil you – Don't be an ass all your life, Toby – This is officer Sean Carter, what's your relationship with Annaliese Miller – Sir? Sir, are you still there?

I closed my eyes and tried to imagine something different; then opened them to enjoy where I was at that moment. I thought of the date, the current time, and what I did that day. After a couple of deep breaths, I was able to look around at my property and live in the current moment. I watched a deer just a few feet in the woods lift its head up.

Click, whoosh, click. Beep—beep—beep beep—beep beep—beep —beep. How are the book ideas coming? Maybe it would be better to let it come to you instead of chasing after a plot. Kiss me one more time, Toby, please.

That's the moment the idea hit me. "HA!" I shouted. The sound startled the deer and it ran away into the woods. I decided on writing a memoir and sharing my story about Anna. *It's not fiction*, I thought to myself, but it was something that would keep me busy; a way to pull the emotion out and put it on the pages of a book. I needed the vivid memories to get out of my head. It would be an emotional toll, but I could use the notes from my journal as a basis, starting with the phone call with Anna when I teased her about the night I had planned for her.

I went back inside, closed the sliding doors behind me, got my backpack and pulled out the laptop. I thought about if I had everything I needed to let the emotions come flooding back just one more time.

I recalled the timeline from the first phone call to the time I left the hospital.

I left the hospital—I left the hospital and—something was given to me. What the hell was it? Ah, a plastic drawstring bag. But what was in it? It was—it was a—was it pamphlets? I walked outside and put it in the back of the truck. When I got home – or was it the next day that I got it out of the back of the car? I put it—I—Oh my God, I never opened it.

I walked back amid the boxes and opened the top on every one of them until I saw the white, crinkled round top with strings hanging down to its side. I lifted it out of the box and set it on the counter. With two fingers from each hand inside the top of the bag, I pulled it open without looking. I took another sip of beer and sighed before looking down at the contents.

Tears fell instantly when I saw the clothes she wore that night still folded neatly; skin tight jeans, a low-cut, black shirt and matching undergarments. I pulled them out of the bag and set them on the granite countertop. My nose caught the scent of her perfume still lingering on her clothing. I pulled them up to my nose and smiled with my eyes closed.

"What the hell was that!" I said as I turned around as quickly as I could after I felt a cold breeze on my neck from behind me. I dropped the clothes on the bar instantly when I felt it. I looked around intently and studied the kitchen by extending my hand near the window, then under the cabinets feeling for a draft; nothing. I walked towards the front door doing the same. Still, I felt nothing. I walked over to the sliding doors and looked into the kitchen. There was nothing that would cause a draft like that. I slowly looked into my room through the already open French doors, listening as the floor squeaked in some places. I walked through the galley kitchen and felt nothing. I walked over towards the basement door. Still, nothing.

I sighed deeply and returned to the kitchen counter, looking over my shoulder occasionally. I picked up Anna's clothes again and looked around with them up to my nose, smelling her intoxicating perfume until I put them back on the counter and said, "Anna? – Sweetheart, was that you?" There was no response.

I reached in the bag again and pulled out her small purse with her tiny wallet, the registration for the vehicle, some spare change and a small blanket that she kept in the trunk during the cold months. I opened the zipper to her wallet. On the right side was three bank cards. On the left, there were some retail loyalty cards. I opened the large pocket on the right to find twenty-four dollars. The pocket on the left had a few loose things, but one item, in particular, caught my attention. It was a business card with a mountain logo on the top left, a slogan across the top that read, YOUR SMOKY MOUNTAIN REALTOR. I knew Anna had been in contact with a few realtors from the area, but I thought it was limited to email updates. The card itself didn't surprise me as much as the name, ALEX REAGAN. I pulled out my phone and compared the number to the one on the card.

"865—"

I matched each digit in my mind after reading the area code aloud. *Have they ever spoken? If so, how often?* I added her last name to Alex's contact card in my phone, then set my phone on the counter. I walked back to the bedroom with Anna's clothes up to my nose in my right hand and was looking down at the business card in my left. I put the clothes on the bed, the card on my nightstand and went back to the office to start writing; but I couldn't focus.

She told me not to look for her. How does Anna know Alex?

I closed the laptop, turned on some lights in the house and went out to the garage to hang up the electronic dartboard for something else to focus on. I used the internet on my phone to look up the official measurements of bullseye height and throwing line. I played music on my phone through a small clock radio as I measured each regulation, hung the board and put blue painter's tape on the floor at the throwing line. When I was done, I opened the dartboard cabinet and turned it on. It powered on with a jingle and I pushed the player button. The little built-in speaker announced, "Two Players." I pushed it again, "Three Players." I pushed it six more times until it announced, "One Player." I pushed another button to start the game and the board announced, "Player One." I played the game called 301. I hadn't played darts in at least a year so I was lucky to hit the board with all three darts in my first round. The third one even prompted the board to announce, "Bullseye" when it landed in the outer center ring, then announced, "Next player." I walked up to the board, pulled the darts out and pushed the button for the next player. "Player One," the board announced.

My mind wandered in so many different directions.

How did Anna get a business card from Alex? How long has she had it? How much did they talk? Does Alex know that Anna was my wife?

"Okay, here's what's going on." I said aloud before I threw a dart. "Anna signed up to get information about real estate in the area. I know this because she showed me properties that were in her email."

"Double Bullseye"

"Woo Hoo!" I threw my arms up with one dart left in my hand and turned around as though there was a crowd of people watching me. "Focus, Tobias." I stopped turning and put my arms down. "One of the real estate companies just happened to be the one Alex works for and some minimum wage, administrative person sent letters to all their contacts and included business cards." I threw the last dart.

"Next Player."

I pulled the three darts out and pushed the button.

"Player One."

"And that's it. They never spoke and Anna really has no idea who Alex is."

A weather alert came across my phone indicating strong storms that would pass through overnight and rain all day the next. I turned off the dartboard, closed it, shut everything off in the garage, locked it up and went back into the house.

My mind shifted to the storms. *Follow your dream of landscape photography.* Rainy days present some of the greatest opportunities for dramatic photographs.

With the storms coming overnight, it will give the rain a chance to saturate the waterfalls and cascades by morning. Based on the temperatures, if the ground is warmer than the air, there might be fog. If the cloud cover is really low, it could be clear up on Newfound Gap and Clingmans' Dome to capture the mountains from above the clouds.

I gathered all of my photography equipment from the office and set it aside for the next morning. My plan was to get up before sunrise and be in the park at first light, even though it would be cloudy. I set my alarm for 6:00, showered and laid down for the night facing Anna's pillow.

I tried with everything I had to not think about the chills in the shower and the creaking of the house the night before or the air on my neck that afternoon.

"I sure hope you're not here, Anna. You made me promise not to find you. If it is you, baby, please; you have to let go. Don't stay here for me, sweetheart."

I placed my hand on her pillow.

"I will always love you. Goodnight, baby."

Chapter 9

House of Pain

A loud crack of Thunder woke me up around 2:30 a.m. I sat up and watched frequent lightning strikes light up the house. Some were partnered with rolling thunder that echoed from mountain to mountain and others just flashed like a strobe. I got a glass of milk from the kitchen using only the flashes from nature's lightshow to see. I drank half the glass standing by the kitchen counter, facing the back door and watched as the porch and tree line lit up.

I heard the floor creak from my right around the end of the stone wall. My heart raced and I quickly realized that a house like this will make sounds on occasion and that's just to be expected. Besides, I was too tired to really care, so I went back to bed with the rest of my milk and watched out the sliding door as the hot tub lit up time after time.

As I laid there, I got an uneasy feeling; like I was being watched. I slowly looked around the room with just my eyes. I tried to look down past my feet, but I wasn't positioned to be able to. Like a minute hand on a clock, I ever-so-slowly turned my head upwards while still looking down towards the end of the bed. The rain poured on the roof and I heard a creaking board that sounded like it was in the kitchen. It didn't just creak once and stop. The sound was as though someone was standing on the board, shifting their weight. I heard a long creak, then a short one, a high-pitched one that was more like a squeak, then a long one again. The open French doors were barely in my view when the house lit up again, making everything visible all the way to the galley kitchen by the stone wall.

I realized just how silly my thoughts were; not to mention my sneaky peek through my bedroom doors. I leaned up on my elbow, drank the rest of my milk, took a deep breath, rolled back to my side and closed my eyes.

My alarm woke me up quickly blasting some heavy music that I didn't recognize. I showered right away, got dressed and put on rain gear and waterproof boots. I gathered my camera pack and tripod, went downstairs and put it in the truck. I opened the garage door and reached behind my seat to make sure I had my umbrella.

The rain was loud when it started pounding on the roof of the truck as I backed out of the garage. The sound moved from the back of the roof to the front and I turned my wipers on when the rain reached my windshield. The rain was steady but wasn't accompanied by storms. I accessed the park from the Greenbrier entrance since it was the closest. There was a place I had in mind a couple of miles in. It was a wooden bridge that went over Porters Creek immediately after a left turn. I could set up my tripod on the bridge to shoot upstream.

I crossed over the one-lane bridge and parked on the right side, then got my umbrella and camera equipment out of the back. I can imagine I looked like an amateur juggler holding the open umbrella in the pocket of my neck and fumbling around with my backpack to get my camera out and set it on the tripod. I had just gotten everything set up as I wanted it and decided to keep my camera pack in the hatchback. Part of the way to the truck, I heard another vehicle coming. With my camera around my neck, I quickly walked back to the bridge to move my tripod, allowing the car to pass. I kept all of the equipment with me and decided to get it all prepared under the protection of the hatchback instead of holding my umbrella between my head and shoulder. The process was far more difficult without Anna.

"Sorry, dear. I guess I never thanked you for all the times you held the umbrella for me." I said sheepishly.

I spent time behind the truck ensuring I had the right filter and lens on the camera. I looked over at the flowing water, then at the camera, adjusting the settings as closely as possible, and then returning to the bridge.

The creek was surrounded by rhododendron, not yet in bloom and the Flame Azaleas lower to the ground offered a stunning highlight to the lush green. The rain was loud on my umbrella and drips turned to trickles at each point. I looked down at the preview on the back of the camera and set the shutter speed for 5 seconds to get a smooth flow of water. I made a few adjustments and took several more shots until I captured exactly what I was hoping for.

The rain made the details of the foliage fade into the distance at the bend in the creek; the contrast of the white rapids against the dark stream popped perfectly. The bright red of the Fire Azaleas against the evergreen leaves of the rhododendron added just enough vibrancy that I was satisfied with the capture to pack everything up and move on to another place.

I drove deeper into the park towards the trailhead for Ramsey Cascades, pulled over to check out a few places, but didn't see anything that I wanted to capture that day. I turned around at the trailhead and drove the four bumpy miles on the dirt road back the way I came in and drove through Gatlinburg.

When I passed stoplight ten and entered the park, an unexpected thought entered my mind; Alex. Looking around at the charred trees, I wondered how she was affected by the fires. I thought about riding with her a few days prior and how we bantered back and forth and how she comforted me; an effortless connection.

I continued past the Chimney Tops picnic area all the way up to Newfound Gap. The cloud cover was still thick. I considered going up to Clingmans Dome, so I pulled out my phone to see the elevation difference. At just shy of a 1,600 feet difference, I decided it wasn't enough to capture the mountains from above the clouds, like I wanted to for so long. I started back down the mountain, stopping occasionally to capture some random waterfalls that didn't exist without a heavy rain.

The sound of the rain and the lack of sleep the night before had me yawning, and it was only a little after noon. I shot a few scenes that day and there was no reason for why I couldn't go back out later in the afternoon, so I went home. By the time I got upstairs with my camera bag, I was excited to download the pictures to see if there was anything worth posting on my photography site. I went to the kitchen to make a sandwich while the pictures were downloading, then went back and sat down at my desk under the window facing out the front of the house.

The first series I looked at was the one I took at the first place I stopped that morning, on the bridge over Porters Creek.

"Too bright—too dark—damn, this one's out of focus a little. Hmm—Oh, wow!"

I found the series towards the end; the ones I got excited about when I saw them on the preview screen on the back of the camera. The way the last one looked on the twenty-seven-inch monitor was stunning. I exported it to my editing software and zoomed in on the photograph where I could only see small sections at a time. I looked for things that made the image look 'dirty,' like dead trees, broken branches, branches that are sticking out of the creek and anything else that could easily be cleaned up.

I zoomed back out on occasion, looking at the photograph in its entirety. When I finished the first draft of cleanup, I stood up from my desk and walked around the room once, looking at the photograph from a distance.

That's when I saw the headlights. There was a car at the end of my gravel driveway with its headlights pointing towards my house. I squinted as I peered out the window at the distorted car from the rain still pouring down. I ran down to the garage and got my umbrella out, opened the front door and walked out to the covered porch. I turned around when I closed the door and froze.

I walked out slowly with the umbrella over my head and with

thoughts racing through my mind with every step. Although I was still a distance from the car, it didn't appear that there were any passengers at all. I approached cautiously and knocked on the window at the same time as I called her name, "Alex?"

She looked up at me and had her hand over her mouth, crying.

"Are you okay?" I asked.

She rolled her window down only about an inch and I held the umbrella over her door. She rolled it down more without speaking.

"Come inside," I offered.

"No, there's no need," she said through sniffles. "I should go."

"Alex, please, just pull up in front of the porch and I'll be right there—please."

She looked through the windshield and back at me. She dropped her head, then out her windshield again, wiping tears from her eyes.

"Please." I repeated, then began to chuckle. "I've been in the house alone for days. If it wasn't for singing along with music and talking to myself, I wouldn't even know what my voice sounded like anymore—please."

She put her window back up and drove slowly to the spot right in front of the entrance to the house. I caught up to her and put my umbrella over the door again and opened it. I offered her my hand. She took it, stepped out of the car and I kept the umbrella over her as we stepped up on the porch and through the front door. She stepped to the side so I could close the front door. She continued to cry and stared at the floor.

"Alex, please. What's going on?"

She wiped her eyes again and said, "Can we sit down?"

I placed my hand gently on her back and said, "Of course, please make yourself at home," and outstretched my arm pointing towards the dining room table. I pulled out the chair at the head of the table for her and she sat.

"Can I get you something to drink? Coffee? Lemonade?"

"Do you have anything stiffer?" she said with a laugh and a sniff.

"Of course, I do, who do you think I am anyway?" I retorted.

I mixed both of us a drink and sat down in the chair next to her. I sipped my drink and watched her as she looked around the house.

"Wow, Toby, you've done great with this place."

I looked around myself and said, "Thanks. I still have some fine-tuning to do." I turned around to see her pulling the empty glass from her mouth and placing it on the table. She had her eyes closed but opened them slowly. I didn't even offer that time. I took her glass and made her another.

"Can I get you anything else?" I asked as I sat back down.

"No, this is fine, thank you."

"Can you tell me what's going on?"

"Toby," she paused. "Do you remember when you were explaining this house to me?"

"Yes," I said.

"Did I act strangely to you?"

"Yeah, I guess a little. I'm assuming it's because I described it so vividly."

She laughed slightly, "Well—there's that."

I reached my hand out to hers across the table. "Alex, what is it?"

She began, "I was the caretaker of this house since it's been empty."

"Well, you certainly did a great job at it."

"I know this house well. I came over here nearly every weekend to spend time with my sister. Man, we would laugh so hard."

She sipped her drink.

"My brother-in-law worked second shift and was never around when I came over. That's the only way I would come over, is if he wasn't here—fucking bastard."

I listened to her story without interruption.

"She was abused, both physically and mentally. He didn't know I came over so much. He didn't allow it."

"He didn't let you visit your own sister?"

"No."

"Why the hell did *she* allow it?"

"He was controlling and—what you have to understand is that it's an incredibly slow process. It started years ago when she and I would go out. He would be all sad and tell her that he just wanted to spend time with her; just the two of them, since they didn't get to spend time together through the week. Back then, we would go out anyway. When she came home, he would hang all over her and tell her how much he missed her and that he was so lonely while she was gone. All of it made her believe that he was so loving.

After a while, he would make plans for the two of them to do something on the night she and I went out. We went three weeks in a row without seeing each other. We just talked on the phone. When she finally confronted him about it, he got angry. It wasn't obvious to begin with, he just made comments about how Saturdays were the only night they had to spend by themselves and he would prefer to spend it with her."

She shook her head and stared at her glass before taking another sip.

"As more time passed, he got more controlling, but it still wasn't obvious to my sister. He wanted to shop with her or by himself while she stayed home. I saw the signs, but she wouldn't hear of it. She just told me that it was because he loved her so much and she was lucky that she had a guy who would shop for her while she stayed home."

"It seems obvious to me and it sounds like it was to you too; wasn't it?" I asked.

"Of course, it was, from an outsider's view, but until the controlled see it for themselves, there's nothing anybody can do. You can't make them believe what you know is true. The more you try to make them believe, the more they pull away, which draws them that much closer to the abuser.

One night, I just showed up when I knew he was working because I hadn't heard from her in a few days. She tried to hide her black eye from me, then made excuses when I saw it. She told me she fell out of bed and hit it on the corner of the nightstand. I yelled at her and told her that if she really thought I would believe that then there's nothing I could do for her."

"I'm so sorry to hear this. So, this was their house?"

"Yes, until—"

She started crying again. I reached my hand out to hers again.

"Until what, Alex?"

"They got into a fight over me one night. I was on the phone with her and he screamed, 'who, the fuck, are you talking to now?'"

I shook my head in disgust.

"She just kept yelling 'No.' His voice got louder, and he said, 'Is it that useless fucking sister of yours?'"

She cried harder and I got a roll of toilet paper for her to use as tissue and placed it on the table. I walked up behind her and put my hands on her shoulders. She took a few deep breaths and continued, "That's when I heard the gunshot."

"Oh, my God, Alex."

"She dropped the phone and I started screaming. He said, 'This is your fucking fault, you know.'—I heard a cabinet door open. It creaked, and I heard my sister call him a son of a bitch and then heard another gunshot. I heard the crashing of pots and pans and a thud. I screamed harder and then I heard my sister's voice—She said, 'I'm so sorry, Alex. I'm so sorry.'"

I used my left hand to pull my lower eyelids down to keep myself from crying, too.

"I heard her breathing, but she never said another word. I called 911 and drove over here as fast as I could, but it was too late."

She stood up and turned around, crying into my shoulder.

"I'm so sorry, Alex."

When she got control of herself, she said, "Look, if you don't want to stay here, I'll give you every penny back that you paid for the house and show you others."

"Not a chance," I said. "How long ago did all that happen?"

"A year ago, today."

I thought of the sounds I'd heard the previous few days. I thought of the chills I got in the shower; the air on the back of my neck and the creaking I heard from the kitchen. As I held her, I looked around the house over her shoulder, then thought of the dowsing rods, the crystal and the spirit box that Anna and I bought in Gettysburg.

I felt her relaxing and began to pull away. She got more tissue from the roll and said, "I am so sorry. I have no business barging in like this. It's your house now and I—"

"It's okay," I said. "You don't worry a bit about it, okay?"

I gently placed my curved finger under her chin and she lifted her eyes to mine.

"Okay?" I repeated with wide eyes.

She smiled, hugged me again and said, "Okay."

"Another drink?" I asked as I pulled her chair out again.

"One more won't hurt, I recon."

She sat down, and I collected her glass to make another. As I walked towards the kitchen, I asked, "Can I ask you a question?"

"Of course."

I leaned on the bar with both of my hands, "Why are you here?"

I was disappointed in my choice of words so I continued, "That sounded awful, I'm sorry. What I'm asking is, what did you hope to accomplish by coming here?"

"I don't really know, I guess. Trying to put it behind me. Trying to move past it. This last year has been awful. I'm sure you understand, right?"

"Of course, I do—to some extent, I suppose. I mean, Anna hasn't even been gone for two months yet."

She turned around in her chair, "How do you do it, Toby?"

"Do what exactly?"

"Carry on every day. I took almost three months off of work when Sara died."

"Sara?" I asked.

"Yes, well, actually, her name was Seraphina."

"That's a beautiful name."

"Yes, it is. So, what's your secret? How is it so easy for you?"

I sat down and put our glasses on the table. "First of all, I don't think 'easy' is a fair word to use. It hasn't been easy at all. Some days are better than others. I made a promise to her before she died. I promised I would live my life. I would carry out our dreams, you know? Maybe the difference is that I got a chance to say goodbye, then essentially, ran away."

"What do you think it would be like if you didn't move?"

"Oh, shit, Alex, I don't even want to think about it. It was awful. Every day was awful up until last week when I came down here. Now I'm in a new place that I've never been to with her. It's hard to drive around the park. I see her everywhere, like I mentioned in the car the other day to you. I call them ghosts of the past and memories of once upon a time."

"I see them too," she said.

I thought again about the chills, the creaking and the air on my neck. "What do you mean, you see them?"

"Like you're saying, the ghosts of the past. They've faded over time. I think it's a result of being the caretaker of this place for the last year, but I imagine us laughing there at the bar and having drinks out on the patio. It's like I can see us."

She looked around again and said, "To be honest, I've never felt so comfortable here than I do right now. It doesn't look the same. You've got your stuff in here now. I think, for the first time, I can begin to let it go, you know? This isn't her house anymore. If I was still the caretaker and was here every day, I think I would probably get more used to it. Maybe someday, I'll be able to think of this place and only remember the good times again."

"I lost both of my parents, years ago. Grieving is a process with many steps that you can't skip. You have to accept every step, or you'll never move on to the next one. Sometimes, things suck, and you just have to let them."

She laughed, "Really? That's your grand advice? Sometimes things suck?"

"Yes, actually, it is. If you ignore it, it will still suck at some point. It will always come back. I found the best way to get rid of the ghosts of the past is to create new memories in familiar places."

She smiled and said, "What exactly are you saying, Toby?"

"I'm just saying that you're welcome here any time. If you want to drown out the memories or just feel closer to your sister, you come over any time."

"Thank you. Sincerely, Toby, thank you for that."

"The only thing I ask is that you call or text first so I'm not just walking around here naked," I smirked

She laughed again and said, "I'll be sure to do that."

Chapter 10
Contact

She finished the last swallow of her drink, stood up from her chair and walked to the sliding glass door. "Looks like the rain is starting to lighten up."

I stood up and walked next to her. "Yeah, it looks that way."

"Thanks again, Toby. This just means the world to me."

I started walking towards the front door slowly and she followed, just as I had hoped. I opened the door and told her, "I meant it, you call any time. If you don't mind, please let me know you made it home safely."

She hugged me one last time before turning to walk out the front door. I stood on the porch to see her off. With a wave out her window, she turned off the gravel drive, onto the road and out of sight.

I ran inside, closed and locked the door behind me then immediately went into the closet to get the equipment. I took the box out to the dining room table and set it down. I pulled the top off and immediately pulled out the dowsing rods; long, skinny brass rods that bend in an "L" at the back with long, brass cylinders barely larger than the rods that are used to hold onto. The cylinders allow the long rods that point straight out to pivot freely and are nearly impossible to control. Holding them in my hand made me remember when we did a ghost hunt at the Cashtown Inn at Halloween.

Our guide, a medium, told us there was an entity in the room and asked us if one of us wanted to try to communicate. I volunteered immediately and told her that I was skeptical about the use of the rods. I had tried them before with no success. She agreed, and I asked Anna for the rods. The medium coached me through the process.

"Try to hold the rods so that they're both pointing straight in front of you."

I did what she asked, which was far more difficult than I imagined. I tried hard to turn the rods by adjusting my hands, but they flopped around.

"Here, use your thumbs to steady them and hold them so very still."

I got her approval when they stopped moving, and she said, "Now you can relax and take your thumbs away, but don't move the rods around."

I did as she said, and she whispered, "Go ahead, ask some questions. They have to be closed-ended questions with just yes or no answers. If the answer is yes, the rods will cross and if the answer is no, they'll separate."

"How do they know that?" I asked.

She smiled and said, "This one has used them before."

She stepped away and I asked my first question, "Is someone in here with us?"

You could have heard a pin drop on the carpet as I stared at the rods, barely swaying a quarter inch to each side. I took a deep breath but held my hands as still as I could. I was skeptical, not a non-believer. Eight other people were in the room with us that night in addition to the medium, and all of them were staring at the tips of those two brass rods.

A woman gasped lightly. The rods crossed slowly, stayed for two or three seconds, then separated again, pointing straight out in front of me.

"Do you stay here all the time?"

I smiled when the rods crossed again. One woman in the room covered her open mouth in awe.

"Did you fight in the war?"

The rods separated. I was disappointed, but still intrigued by the contact I was making. I couldn't think of any more questions, so I stopped and handed the rods back over to Anna. She didn't hesitate.

"Hi, my name is Anna, are you still here?"

The rods crossed instantly.

"Was it you who walked next to my bed last night?"

All ten of us were intently focused on the rods when she asked, and even more when they crossed again.

"I thought so, but you're not going to hurt us, are you?"

The rods separated, and Anna put the dowsing rods away as one gentleman in the room with us said, "Oh, hell no," and walked out of the room.

I put the rods down on the table and reached back into the box to find the crystal, which also only works with closed-ended questions but a 'Yes' response is signified by the tip of the crystal moving in a circular motion and with a 'No' response, the crystal swings from side to side. I carefully laid the crystal on the table and gently laid the fine chain that it hangs from out to its side. I reached back in to get the spirit box, a frequency transmitter that makes it possible to hear the entity talking in real-time through static and white noise.

Our first experience with a spirit box was another sponsored paranormal investigation. We had the box turned on and were sitting at a dining room table. The only light was from a few flashlights in the entire house. Anna and I were the only ones in that room.

I started with, "Is there anybody here?" We immediately heard a small child laugh in the midst of the static.

"What's your name?"

We didn't get a response and after more than ten minutes of trying, our guide suggested we just talk to each other and not try to make contact. He claimed that they needed to build trust in us.

We started talking and heard the small child again. Anna smiled at me and leaned closer to the box.

"Hi, my name is Annaliese, who's this?

There was an immediate response from a man's voice that said, "Anna?"

I slapped my hand on the table and said, "Holy shit, babe, did you hear that?"

Anna simply smiled and nodded her head.

I placed the spirit box on the table and put the empty cardboard box on the floor. I picked up the dowsing rods first and walked to the middle of the living room with steady hands.

"Is there anyone in here with me?"

I focused entirely on the brass rods, but they didn't move. I walked through the house and repeated the same question several times. Each time, the rods stayed ever so still. That's when I realized that if there was an entity in the house with me, it was quite unlikely that they would have any idea of what to do with those skinny, brass rods. I spoke clearly and slowly.

"If there's anyone in here with me, these are called dowsing rods. They won't hurt you. Because I'm holding them, you can use my energy to move them. I'm going to ask some questions. If the answer is yes, make the rods cross over each other, and if the answer to my question is no, then pull them apart."

I felt a chill pass over me, but I couldn't tell if it was from my own adrenaline or if it was—something else.

"Is there someone in here with me?"

The rods were pointing straight out in front of me. The tip of the one on the left started to sway so slightly that it was barely noticeable.

I whispered, "That's it, you can do it. If you're here, cross the rods over each other."

The right one began to move, then both of them slowly started to pivot in the cylinders randomly, like a small child struggling to put a block in its place. They swayed in the same direction, both pointing to the right, then as sure as you're reading this right now, the right one started pivoting to the left and they both stopped, perfectly crossed over each other without touching.

I got a sensation all over me as every hair on my body stood up and I questioned whether I wanted to continue or not. I straightened the rods and held them steady with my thumbs then slowly lowered my thumbs around the cylinders.

"Sara?"

They slowly started pointing in different directions, then went straight again after only slight movement. I waited without saying a word. The rods continued to sway, then they crossed.

I smiled and said, "Hi Sara—my name is Toby." I had hundreds of questions, but asked the first that I wanted to know, "Was it you that caused me to get chills in the shower?"

The rods crossed.

"And the air on the back of my neck?"

They crossed again.

"Were you in the kitchen during the storm last night?"

She confirmed.

"Is your husband here too?"

The rods flew open so fast and without hesitation that they swung all the way back and bounced off my upper arm, which startled me. My heart beat faster. I steadied the rods and sighed before I continued, "Does Alex know you're here?"

No.

I straightened the rods and asked one more question, "Are you angry?"

No

I put the rods down and paced around the house. My phone vibrated on my hip. It was a text from Alex.

Thank you again. You're very
kind. I made it home.

You're welcome, Alex. It was
nice to spend some time with
you. I'd like to do it again
sometime.

I'd like that too, but next time,
no tears.

You've got yourself a deal.

I picked up the rods again, walked out to the living room and said, "Sara, I'm so sorry for what happened to you. Nobody deserves that. I wish you could have seen the signs earlier so it didn't escalate so horribly, and I sincerely hope that you can find peace someday."

I walked into the kitchen and asked, "Can I talk to you again sometime?"

The rods didn't move. I set them down on the counter and looked around, trying to replay the events of a year before in my mind. I looked into the galley kitchen and imagined him walking through it with a pistol drawn. I looked down at the corner cabinet behind me and imagined Sara laying there. I reached down for the cabinet handle and slowly opened it—creak—squeak—creak.

An eerie feeling washed over me, and I walked through the kitchen, into the office to finish editing the pictures I took that morning.

I sat down at my desk, unlocked the screen and sighed as my shoulders dropped.

"Great! I live in a haunted house."

My mind flickered between Alex's visit, the story she told me, the contact with Sara and the photographs I took that day. I needed something to focus on and decided to try to start writing again.

I started the memoir with a poem, then jumped right into my reaction when I got the phone call from Officer Carter. I brainstormed several ways to start writing them all out and would decide later which I like the most.

~~It was late in March when I got the call. My wife had been out with her friends.~~

~~It's strange how life can change in an instant. One minute I was planning a romantic evening for my wife and the next I was racing to the hospital.~~

~~I kissed my wife goodbye that night, never expecting it would be the last time.~~

~~"Tobias Miller, this is Officer Sean Carter."~~

I finally decided on the last one I wrote.

I froze when I heard the news. I couldn't believe it. I was stunned into silence; truly shocked. My heart sank as my back hit the wall with a thud, my knees buckled, and I slowly slid down the wall. My knees met my chest with the phone still pressed to my ear.

I kept writing after the last entry and deleted the others. It broke my heart to take my mind back to that night, but I felt as though I had to keep writing. I opened my music software and turned the volume down so that I could still think. Instead of playing music that Anna hated, I turned on our playlist that we listened to all the time. When I clicked the button to shuffle all of the songs, the first one that came on was an old country song from Joe Diffie, "A Night to Remember."

The only light on in the house was the glow of my computer monitor. I sang along with some of the songs as I wrote line after line, laughing through tears at some places and, eventually, I found myself nodding off when I re-read sections that I had just written.

I went to bed and touched the pillow on the other side.

"Goodnight, Anna."

I rolled over onto my back.

"Goodnight, Sara."

Chapter 11

Learning to Live

I went shopping the next day for rocking chairs for both the front and back porches and picked up a couple of chairside tables. I also got some plastic chairs for the hot tub area and some gasoline for the lawn mower and four-wheeler. When I pulled up to the house with the trailer, I noticed how long the grass had gotten and figured that should be my first order of business for the day.

With my mp3 player, I did the trimming first, then used the push mower for the perimeter before using the new riding mower. The lawn was lush, and the smell of freshly cut grass filled the air. As I got towards the middle of the tree line, I noticed a wide gap in the trees, leading into the woods and thought that Alex could tell me about the borders of the property. How much was mine? I had no idea.

When I finished, I hosed off the mower and put it away, went inside and called Alex.

"Well, hey, Toby, how are you?"

Oh, that accent just made me melt just a little more every time I heard it.

"I'm good, Alex, how are you?

"I'm hanging in there, what's up?"

"Sometime when you have a chance, I'm wondering if you could come back over and show me the boundaries of the property—unless it's something you can tell me on the phone."

"So, you're saying you'd prefer that I tell you over the phone instead, so you don't have to see me?"

"Oh, my God, Alex; that's not at all what I'm saying. I'm just—if you have stuff going on—" I sighed and shook my head at my foolish choice of words and listened to her laughing at her own cleverness. "I'm saying that sometime when you don't have other appointments, I would greatly appreciate it if you came over to show me the boundaries of the property."

"I'm actually done with my appointments for the day."

"Oh, it doesn't have to be today if you have other things you need to do."

"Toby?"

"Yes, ma'am."

"Shut up. I'm happy to come show you. Some of it is easier to get to with a four-wheeler so I can show you some today and—"

"I have a four-wheeler."

"Well then; I can show you all of it today. I'm surprised you're not in the park on such a beautiful day like today."

"It's time to start paying attention to my home and finish getting settled in."

"When do you want me?"

How about right after a few drinks?   I laughed at myself.   "It doesn't matter to me, whenever it's good for you."

"What's so funny?" she asked.

I dramatically said, "Oh, nothing."

"Tobias Miller. Don't make me come down there."

"Ooh, somebody drank a glass of sassy this morning, didn't they?"

She laughed and I finally answered her, "Any time is good for me, so whenever you can make it will be perfect."

"Let's see, it's about 11:30 now. I can be there in twenty minutes."

I confirmed and we ended the call. I quickly looked around the house and got the dowsing rods off the counter and put them in the box that was still on the floor along with the crystal and the spirit box. I took another lap around the house to make sure I didn't have anything left out, and opened doors all around, allowing the smell of the mountain air to fill the house.

Everything looked good, except the pile of clothes in the corner of my room behind one of the French doors. I use the term 'corner' loosely. I wish they actually were in the corner, but they weren't. They were up against the clothes basket that *was* in the corner. I lifted the lid to the basket and said, "Of course," when I noticed it was empty. I put the clothes into the basket and quickly made the bed.

I looked out the front door at least ten times over the next few minutes.

What are you doing, man? Relax, it's just a visit. Does everything look okay? Maybe I should offer her something to drink when she comes in? Shit, I don't have anything except Diet Mountain Dew, beer, and some liquor. What the hell is in this pantry?

I walked over and opened the skinny door between the kitchen and the front door.

Canned shit, more canned shit, bread, peanut butter, cereal, more canned shit—Ah! Lemonade mix.

I filled a two-quart pitcher more than halfway with ice, filled it with water, put in the powdered mix and stirred it. I put the spout up to my mouth and sampled it.

"Damn, that's good," I said and put it in the refrigerator. I walked up to the front window again, anxiously waiting for her to show up, then decided I should at least *try* to look like I'm not nervous. I put some ice in a glass and poured myself some of the lemonade and sat in one of the rocking chairs on the front porch. I pulled my cell phone from my belt clip with one hand and pushed the button to see the time. It had been twenty-three minutes.

I took a deep breath and closed my eyes, focusing on the sound of the chirping birds, the smell of freshly-cut grass, the warmth of the day and the taste of the lemonade on my tongue as I rocked back and forth. I heard tires on gravel and opened my eyes to see her pulling in.

Should I stand up and greet her? Stay sitting right here?

She waved as she approached and I smiled and waved back, still rocking slowly in my chair. She opened the car door to get out. She was wearing a white shirt with lace around the neck. Her jean shorts hugged her curves perfectly and her brunette hair seemed to shimmer in the sunlight. She walked towards me and looked down, shyly, with a smile, and ran her fingers through her hair to pull it to the side. Her skin was so smooth and her legs; oh, those legs.

I put my lemonade on the little table between the chairs and stood up when she reached the steps. She hugged me when she reached the top. That's when I noticed the smell of her perfume that made me have to compose myself before pulling away so that she wouldn't notice how it affected me and she spoke, "You sure look comfortable with your rocking chair and your lemonade."

"That's why I'm here." I looked around, "It's perfect."

"Here, this is for you," she said as she handed me a bottle of Merlot. "Thank you again for last night. I think I slept more peacefully than I have in a year. I had to, like you said, accept that part of the process."

"Oh, you didn't have to—"

"I know," she interrupted, then said sincerely, "I wanted to."

I opened the door and allowed her to enter first.

"Can I get you a glass of lemonade?" I asked.

"I'll find my way, thank you. You just sit down there, and I'll take care of the rest."

She opened a few cabinets before finding the one with the glasses. I almost told her where they were but figured that 'Miss Sassy' would have something to say about that. When she finished preparing her own glass, she brought the pitcher over to fill mine and said, "Shall we go outside? It's far too nice to stay in here."

I stood up with my lemonade and walked through the open, sliding screen door. We walked out onto the covered porch and both looked out at the woods.

"I just love this place." I told her

The hot tub motor came on and she looked over at it, "You got the tub running," and walked in to look under the cover.

"Yes, I did." I looked back out to the tree line. "So, how much land is here anyway?"

She closed the cover, walked out, looked towards the back of the property and said, "You're sitting on just under seven acres."

"Seven acres? Really?"

"Oh yeah, it's all wooded, other than right here. The creek runs across the property line through a shallow ravine about a hard stone's throw in. Some of the property is steep and other parts are pretty level. You shoot?"

"I have a few guns, yes. Just for target shooting. I don't hunt."

"Daryl set up a range back there, but it's not more than about a football field in length." She pointed to the right edge of the trees.

"Daryl?"

"Dickhead. My brother-in-law."

"Oh, got it."

"Off to the left there, there's a riding trail that crosses the creek. There's a really nice picnic area back there with a gazebo and candles mounted to the uprights. There's a charcoal grill back there too."

"Well, let's check it out."

She followed me to the garage. I opened the overhead door, filled the four-wheeler with gas and pulled the key out of my pocket.

"Wow, this is nice. You ever operate one of these before?"

"No, ma'am, but I can't imagine it's that hard to figure out."

She looked up at the ceiling, "Oh Lord." She looked back at me and said, "Give me them keys."

"I should have expected this, right?"

"Until you know the land back there, I ain't putting my ass on the back of this thing with you."

She threw her right leg up over the four-wheeler and started it, then turned to me and said, "Well, get on."

I got on the back and held on to the bars on the sides of the seats. No matter how much I tried to keep a little distance, the contour and the angle of the seat made me slide forward right against her. She started out of the garage slowly and turned to the edge of the tree line closest to the garage. We turned to the left to follow the tree line and she slowed down when we turned right into the woods through a wide gap in the trees.

She turned her head to the side a little and yelled back at me, "You gotta be careful when you're back here." I leaned forward so I could hear. "When you drive this thing yourself, you gotta get familiar with the trail. It's not real long, but there are turns that you can't miss, or you'll be hugging a tree *real* tight and you don't want that."

I listened to her instructions and, at the same time, admired the smell of her perfume that was so much stronger while we rode. She sped up at times and slowed down at others to turn along a ridgeline or avoid a large tree. I leaned forward again when she turned her head back and said, "You can't trust the trail, ever. Some of the trees back here are dead and it won't take much of a wind to knock some of these down and block the trail during a storm."

She slowed down again when we approached the creek. I tapped her on the shoulder and asked her to stop. The creek rushed towards us, strongly, from the rain the day before. About fifty yards upstream, I could see a cascade; only about 4 feet tall, but was likely, the cause of the sound I could hear from the back porch. From the place we were, the sound of it was roaring over the idling engine.

"Alex, this is amazing back here."

"The gazebo is just up here a bit."

I held onto the bars again and told her, "Let's go."

We went down into the ravine slowly and right back up the other side. The trail turned to the right and I could see the gazebo ahead of us. When we reached it, she turned the engine off and we walked into the structure. There was seating around the perimeter of it and a two-person swing hanging from the middle. I looked around the gazebo, then out towards the woods, leaning on one of the posts. The sounds of the birds echoed off the trees. I heard leaves rustling beside me from two chipmunks chasing each other. The noise stopped when they ran in a spiral up a tree. I heard a creaking sound behind me. When I turned to look, Alex had just sat down on the swing and patted the empty spot next to her, inviting me to sit.

I sat down carefully and slowly rocked the swing back and forth; neither of us spoke. Only the sounds of nature and the occasional squeak of the swing when it changed direction could be heard. It felt so right, but at the same time, I felt guilty.

"What are you thinking?" she asked.

"Why would I be thinking something?"

"Because we stopped swinging and I've been looking at you for the last two minutes and you haven't moved."

Nothing, I thought to myself, but knew she wouldn't buy that; more today than ever. I took her hand and started, "Can I be straight with you?"

"Of course."

"Alex, I'm not sure what's going on." I pulled both of our intertwined hands up to my heart. "Up here," then put our hands back down. "Ever since you picked me up that day, I've felt connected to you somehow. I can't describe it. You're fun, you're sassy, you're confident, you're—beautiful."

I looked over at her to see how she was taking it in. She smiled sheepishly. "I've known you for less than two weeks and here I am in the middle of the woods, sitting in a gazebo on a swing, holding your hand. The culture here is obviously different than up North where I'm from, I just don't know if I'm reading it all accurately."

"What do you think it is?"

"Well, I guess it feels like you feel the connection too."

"Mhm."

"Alex, I lost Anna two months ago. I haven't been with anyone else in fourteen years. I mean, I don't feel like it's wrong, I just feel —a little guilty, I guess. I just don't know how to feel. I keep hearing Anna in my mind telling me to live while I'm alive, but I don't know how. I think I'm learning, but I'm not done yet."

"Learning to Live?"

"Yeah, I guess. I was so sad until I got here. I just keep reflecting on the process. Am I ignoring part of it and trying to move on too quickly?"

"Do you think you are?"

"I don't know."

She pulled my hand towards her to get my attention, and at the same time, she whispered, "Hey." She placed her right hand up to the side of my face. "Two weeks doesn't erase fourteen years you had with your wife. Two weeks certainly doesn't erase all the time I had with my sister. You and me, we're both learning to live again." She leaned in and kissed me gently. "Maybe we can learn together."

A tingling feeling washed over me. I felt weightless. I put my hand on the side of her face to match hers and we smiled at each other. Her hair blew lightly with the breeze and her hazel eyes danced back and forth looking into mine. I leaned towards her slowly and her smile broadened just before she closed her eyes and our lips met again. She placed the palm of her hand on my chest and I touched my hand on top of hers when I finally spoke, "I'd like that," and kissed her one more time.

I looked around the gazebo again and asked, "Have you ever been out here at night?"

"No," she said softly, "not yet."

We leaned back in the swing and rocked back and forth again.

"Toby, what do you do all day by yourself here?"

"I don't know yet. I haven't even figured that out. Yesterday morning was the first time I left the house for something other than shopping.

"Yesterday was awful, what on Earth did you do in the rain?"

"I'm a landscape photographer and some of my most dramatic, vivid photographs were taken from under an umbrella. Yesterday, I went out to shoot Porters Creek in Greenbrier. I went a few other places too, but I haven't looked at all the pictures I took yet."

"Why don't you have any pictures up in the house?"

"Haven't got there yet. I will."

"Will you show me sometime?"

"Of course, I will."

"What else have you done since you moved in?"

"Yesterday, after you left, I started writing."

"What are you writing?"

I paused for a moment as the last thirty-six hours with Anna flooded my brain in an instant. "A memoir. Anna told me after my first book that I should try fiction, but I never came up with an idea that wasn't already published or that wasn't a terrible idea."

"Terrible?" she laughed. "Like what?"

"I don't know," I chuckled. "more vampires, werewolves, zombies—bullshit that nobody cares about anymore basically. Well, not that people don't care about it, the market is just flooded with it. I want something original."

"And you've written another book?"

"Yes, it's a motivational self-help book about five principles to succeed through change."

"So, you're a motivational writer, a writer of a memoir, a landscape photographer, a carpenter—"

I laughed and said, "You make it sound like I don't know what I want to do when I grow up."

"No, that's not what I'm saying at all, Tobias."

"Tobias?"

"Yes, Tobias. I'm just saying that you're talented. Is there anything else you do?"

"As much as I possibly can. My Mom was my biggest fan and she always told me to learn as many things as I possibly can because you never know what you're going to like. When she passed, Dad went into a deep depression and I knew it wouldn't be long. He died just about six months later."

"What happened to him?"

"Broken heart, I guess. When you devote your entire life to one person, you lose the will to live when that person is gone. I still miss her terribly. I think, all throughout my life, Mom was making sure I was prepared to live without her."

"You were close to your Mom."

"Yes, I was. She believed in me when I couldn't believe in myself. I would tell her that I wanted to do something and she always said I should do it, so ever since then, when I'm interested in something, I try it. Did you see the bookshelves in the living room?"

"Yes, they're beautiful."

"I made them. Anna showed me a few pictures of what she wanted and I designed and built them. I have a drum set and a guitar in the basement. Never really learned the guitar, and I'm not great on the drums, but I'm good enough to play along."

"I could never learn an instrument," she said. "There's just no time."

"Alexandra Reagan!" I scolded.

She looked at me and I continued seriously, "There's no time not to. We are surrounded by death. My Mom and Dad, Anna, Sara, and Daryl—should I go on?"

"No, sir," she said with a grin.

"Alex, there's more to life than what you and I know. We establish our own limits and that's what holds us back. If you want to learn an instrument or climb Mount Everest or—anything—do it. I feel more strongly about that now than ever."

"Perhaps I have more to learn than I thought," she said.

"About what, exactly?"

"Living."

Chapter 12
Secrets

I stood up and used my hand to pull her off the swing. She launched towards me and I caught her with our arms around each other.

"Thank you," she said.

"For what?"

"Just being you, I guess."

"It wasn't really all that difficult if I'm being honest with you," I said sarcastically.

She rolled her eyes and shook her head at me, then asked, "What else do you want to see today?"

"What else do you want to show me?"

She grinned.

"I mean, on the property," I clarified.

"If I show you everything at once, you won't have a reason to invite me back."

"Oh, Alex, I think I have plenty of reasons to invite you back."

We got on the four-wheeler and went back to the house. When I closed the garage door, I said, "I'm going to grab a beer, you want one?"

"Thanks, but I better go before I lose my mind completely."

I didn't have to ask her to clarify what she was talking about. I felt it too. There was an overwhelming sense of excitement, nervousness and, for me, sexual frustration.

"Trust me, I get it." I said. "Thanks for coming over. Thanks for showing me some of the property and—" I opened my arms to her and she stepped forward to fill them. I looked into her eyes and finished, "thanks for letting me open up to you."

I kissed her on the lips twice and she asked, "When do I get to see you again?"

"Friday night. I'll come pick you up and take you out for dinner."

"Ooh, like a date?"

"Ew, a date; that sounds awful after so many years, so formal."

"Awful, Mister?"

"Yes, Alex, a date."

"Okay," she said before turning towards her car. "I'll see you Friday."

I followed her until I reached the porch and walked up the steps. She started the car, smiling the whole time. She rolled her windows down and turned up the radio as she pulled away, bobbing her head to Brett Eldridge, "Something I'm Good At."

I turned around and walked inside the house, closing just the screen door behind me. I was still smiling as I turned on the radio and scanned the stations to try to find the same one Alex was listening to. I found the station, turned the volume up and set the remote down.

When I turned towards the dining room, I gasped, "What the fuck!" The breeze through the house was stronger with both the front and back doors open. The sun was setting but shining brightly on the reflective mahogany table. I inched closer as I replayed the day in my mind, wondering how they got there. There was no way that I would have left them out. Hell, I even sat down at the table while Alex got her lemonade and it was empty. I looked around the house and focused on the gold light halfway up the wall reflecting the sun off the shiny, brass dowsing rods in the middle of the table.

"Do you want to talk?" I asked.

The tip of one of the rods moved slightly.

I reached for the rods and closed all the doors before holding them in my hands. I stood by the dining room table and said, "Are you here?"

They didn't move.

"Sara? Where are you?"

I walked into the living room and turned off the stereo.

"Are you in here?"

I walked around to different areas of the house upstairs, asking questions with no response. I considered that, maybe, it wasn't Sara, so I asked if anyone was in the house with me. I went down to the basement and tried to make contact down there, but still got nothing. I walked back upstairs and into the galley kitchen. A flash of the vision of Sara on the floor in the far corner left my mind as soon as it entered, and I walked through the galley and into the larger kitchen.

"Sara? Anyone?"

I dreaded the answer and wondered if I should even ask the next question that entered my mind, but asked anyway, "Daryl?" I stared at the rods intently and sighed heavily with relief when they didn't move.

I walked over into the dining room and put the rods back on the table, stepped away and asked the first question again, "Do you want to talk?"

Nothing.

I jumped when I heard the sound of static coming from my bedroom. I knew right away where it was coming from. I opened the far closet and reached down to pick up the spirit box that seemed to get louder as I held it. I turned the volume down as I walked out of the room to put it on the mahogany table.

"Sara?"

The static flickered occasionally, but nothing came through. I kept it on and paced through the living room trying to think of a way to make contact.

What does she want? Is she okay? Was it even Sara that was trying to communicate with me?

I circled around the stone wall. The third time around, I finally heard something. It was as clear as the voice Anna and I heard sitting at the table years ago trying to communicate with the little boy.

"Toby."

The hair stood up on my neck and I rushed over to the table.

"Yes, I'm here. Sara?"

I heard occasional sounds within the static, similar to an a.m. radio picking up a distant frequency.

"Sara? Is that you?"

"Yes," I heard quickly. "It's me."

I recognized the accent. Maybe it was just my imagination and the quick response through the static, but she sounded so much like Alex.

"Are you okay?" I asked.

"Yes. I just wanted to—"

"Wanted to do what, Sara?"

A full ten seconds went by before I heard the reply, "to talk to you."

I smiled. It was strange, but I wasn't scared. Somehow, sitting there at that moment talking to the woman who was killed in the house a year before seemed very normal.

"Last night, you said Alex didn't know you were here. Why not?"

"Sad."

"You're sad or she would be?

There was a hesitation between each response like it was difficult for her to communicate, but she answered all my questions.

"Both—Love her—Sister."

"This is amazing, Sara."

"Yes."

"Do you mind if I get a drink?"

"Please do."

I stood up, still smiling, listening to the static from the spirit box, walked over to the kitchen and mixed myself a drink. After the ice dispenser stopped, I heard breaks in the static, then a question, "Can I have one?" followed by laughter.

"Oh, you've got jokes?" I said.

She laughed again. When I finished making my drink, I sat back down at the table.

"It's Alex," she said through the static.

"What is?"

Just then, my phone rang on my hip and I reached for it.

"Off," Sara said.

I reached over and turned off the spirit box, then pulled my phone from its case. Indeed, it was Alex. "Hello," I answered.

"Hey, whatcha doin'?"

"Uh, I—I'm just sitting—"

"It's not a test, Toby, it was just a simple question."

"Oh, we're back to being sassy again, huh?"

"You wouldn't have it any other way."

I stood up and walked around the house, looking out the front door and the windows, "I guess you're right about that. Did you make it home okay?"

"Not yet, I decided to stop by a place I know and wondered if you wanted to meet me."

"You haven't had enough of me today?" I stalled as I considered my situation. Alex was on the phone inviting me out to meet her at the same time as I was just starting to communicate with her dead sister.

"Well, if you don't want to—"

"No, it's not that, I had a really great time today, but maybe Friday night after dinner?"

"That's perfect. I look forward to it," she said.

"Thanks for the invite."

"If you change your mind, you know how to reach me."

"Yes, I do." I said, and we ended the phone call.

I took a deep breath and reached for the spirit box to turn it back on. I heard what sounded like a whimper, then Sara spoke first, "Miss her."

"I bet you do. I miss my wife."

"Anna."

"Yes. You know?"

"Yes—hear everything."

"Of course. You could hear me, but I couldn't hear you. That's not very fair now, is it?"

"No."

Her voice seemed to become more distant, so I asked, "Where are you?" but there was no response. I walked by the front door and turned on the dining room light.

"Here." I heard, then sat back down.

"Are you right here with me at the table?"

"Yes—stay—close."

"You have to stay close to the box to talk to me?"

"Yes."

"How long have you been here?"

"Ever since—"

I didn't want to make her say it, so I interrupted, "I see. Have you seen others?

"Just Alex."

"So, there's no ghost network where you all communicate and talk to each other?"

She laughed and said, "Don't know."

"You've never seen anyone at all?"

"Anna?"

I thought about the promise I made to Anna and felt guilty for even hinting to contact with her.

"I'm sorry, Sara, I just—"

"No."

"No, you haven't seen or heard from her?"

"Toby—let go—hard for us too."

"Hard in what way?"

"Sad."

"Anna told me just before she died that she didn't want me to try to contact her." I thought back on that moment and couldn't tell if it was my imagination or if the conversation really happened. "I think so anyway. She was lying in the hospital bed with black eyes, a bandage on her head and a cast on her left arm. When she spoke to me, it all fell away and she was radiant again as always. Jesus, Sara, I don't even know if it was real. She said it would be too hard for both of us if I tried to contact her. Maybe she was already gone."

"Going," I heard through the static.

"Like, between the two worlds?"

"Yes—I just—"

"You what, Sara?"

"I stayed here."

"So, I couldn't contact Anna even if I tried?"

"Don't know—Toby, don't."

"I won't," I said.

To change the subject, I asked, "Have you been all over the

house?"

"Yes."

"So, you can move about freely wherever you want to?"

She laughed the kind of amorous laugh you would hear from a teenage girl just picked up for a first date.

"What's so funny?" I asked.

"Shower."

"Oh, you're so bad, Sara. The cold chill I felt in the shower; you touched me?"

"Yes—research."

"Research, my ass."

"Yes," she laughed.

"Seraphina!" I said sternly, yet playfully.

"Wanted to know," she said more seriously. "Can you feel?"

"All the times Alex was in here, you never tried to contact her at all?"

"No."

"Why me then?"

"You—only—visitor."

After a brief moment of static, she said, "Lonely."

Her voice was fading again. Even one-word answers were getting broken up. It was such a pleasant and intriguing conversation, I didn't want it to end. There were breaks in the static again as though she was trying to say something. After a minute of static, a single word was audible, "Tired."

"Tired? Do you sleep?"

"No."

"Oh, more like weak?"

"Yes."

"Wait, before you go, I have one more question." I paused, considering how she might take it. "Sara, what do you look like?"

"Alex."

"You look like Alex?"

I barely heard her giggle then she said, "Yes—twin."

"She's your twin?" I said loudly and surprised.

"Long—long-air."

She was breaking up so much I could barely understand her, but I kept trying, "Long? Long air?"

What the fuck is long air?

"Ooh, longer hair?" I said, as though I had just figured out a puzzle and won some elaborate prize.

"Yes."

"Well, Sara, my friend, this has been amazing. Can we talk more sometime?"

"Please."

I paused for a moment then asked, "What do I tell Alex?"

"Nothing," she immediately responded clearly.

"Ok then, it will be our secret."

I waited until Sara stopped responding to turn off the spirit box and said, "Talk to you later, Sara." I felt a cold chill on my left shoulder. It startled me at first, but then I reached my hand up with a smile. I went into the bedroom to turn on the bedside light, then turned off the light over the dining room. I went to the bathroom, brushed my teeth and stripped down to my boxers. When I grabbed the elastic waistband, I looked around the room without pushing them down. I laughed a little at the thought that Sara could see me, got into bed and pulled the covers up to my shoulder. I reached up, turned the light off and got comfortable again.

"Goodnight."

I laid on my left side, facing the sliding door. I could see very little by the glow of the night lights. With my head depressing my pillow, there was very little visible beyond the edge of the pillow and the comforter that had slipped down to my elbow from reaching for the light. Just before I closed my eyes, I felt the sheets shift. I opened my eyes wider and saw them slide up to my shoulder and stretched a little tighter around my body.

"Thank you, Sara."

Chapter 13

Morning Surprise

I was woken up by a subtle, yet annoying sound. It took a while to figure out what it was. I turned over a couple of times, but it wouldn't stop. I finally woke up enough to reach over and pick my vibrating phone up off the nightstand.

"Mm—hello?" I said, sleepily.

"Tobiath—Tob—Tobeee"

"Alex, where are you?"

"Uh, I'm still at the bar," she slurred.

"Dear God, what time is it?"

"Don't know, but they said I can't stay here after they close."

"Alex, put me on speaker."

I heard the phone drop and Alex squeal, then laugh. I heard it switch to speaker and she said, "Sorry, I dropped you."

"Find me in your contacts."

"Mmmm—kay—Oh, look; there you are."

I couldn't help but smile a little. "When you open it, there should be an option part way down the screen to share your location."

"But I can tell you where I am."

"Alex, please, just select the button to share your location."

"Hey, look at that, I did it."

I accepted the notification on my own phone and started navigation to get to her. I set my phone on the bed while I threw on the clothes I was wearing earlier and left to get her.

The whole way to the bar, I kept thinking about making contact with Sara and that I needed to keep it a secret from Alex. I knew she'd be devastated if she found out that her twin was still in the house and having conversations with me. For that matter, she'd be absolutely certain that I had lost my mind. Hell, at that time, I wasn't sure I hadn't. I kept trying to convince myself that the situation was so incredibly different than it would have been if Sara was alive. At the core of the situation was nothing more than being in the early dating stages with Alex and living in a haunted house.

Then the depth of the situation started to become clearer. The ghost in my house was the twin sister of the woman I was attracted to. I had a conversation with her and I wasn't supposed to tell Alex. What's more, my ghastly roommate was in the shower with me, has blown lightly on the back of my neck and even tucked me into bed just earlier that night.

Lonely.

I kept hearing Sara's voice in my mind just like I heard it through the static. *Lonely.* I could relate. Some of the strangest things became the biggest adjustments when Anna died, like putting the coffee pot away and using the single-serve. Looking around the house and only seeing my things made it clear that I was alone. The nights seemed endless, sitting on the couch watching the ghosts of the past moving about the house, then realizing they were only in my mind; mere memories. It's like sitting in a cold, dark theater. The doors are locked and not even the faintest glow can be seen from the stage, yet the theater is somehow alive. You make yourself believe that the stage is filled with actors, and the music surrounds you just like thousands of other guests. Then, eventually, the lights fade, the music stops, and all the people disappear until all that's left is a cold dark building. You're left sitting there alone in silent darkness, wondering if the theater will ever reopen.

Sara had been in a house with no furniture; no memories for a year. The only visitor was the person she loved more than anything in this world but couldn't communicate with her. She couldn't touch her, hug her or talk to her. She could only watch her walk in and out as the caretaker who didn't even know she was there. I imagined her crying in the corner of the house somewhere. Hiding, just to be certain and having to endure the sight and sound of her twin moving about the house, completing chores, walking out, then listening to the deadbolt dramatically slide inside the door frame. I imagined Alex driving away and the house returning to the silent state Sara had been punished with; a heart-breaking price to pay for choosing to stay behind.

I occasionally glanced at the navigation on my phone to ensure I was still going the right way. When I pulled up to the bar, all the lights were off, except the one in the front shining down on the front door. Alex was laying down on a bench, curled in a ball with her feet up and a coat laying on top of her. There was a large man pacing near her talking on his phone and smoking a cigarette when I pulled up parallel to the bench and stepped out. He ended his conversation with laughter before saying in a very strong accent, "He's here. Once she's safely in his car, I'll be on my way."

He turned to me and said, "Toby," he reached his hand out to me with a warm greeting. "I've heard a lot about you. I'm Rick. I own this place."

"She okay?" I asked.

"Oh, she's alright. I shoulda paid more attention to how much she was drinkin', so I apologize for that."

I opened the passenger door and walked over towards Alex.

"Can you git 'er?" he asked.

"Oh, I'll be fine, thanks." I said as I picked her up with her legs draped over my right arm and her head dangling over my left. "This your coat, Rick?"

"Yeah, but you go on. I'll get it from you next time."

"The truck is warm and with the coat, I don't want her to get too warm being in this state, if you know what I mean. Drunk and hot don't go together very well."

Rick laughed and said, "Now, you know that's not a truck, right?" as I handed him the coat when I got her inside.

I looked towards the side of the building and there was a shiny, black pick-up truck that had tires that were as high as my hood, several lights stretched across the top and a large, orange 'T' that covered the back window.

"I know, Rick," is the only thing I could think to reply. "Thanks for taking care of her." I said as I closed her door.

"You must be a hell of a guy, Mister."

I looked at him curiously.

"I knowed Alex a long time. I ain't never heard her talk about no man like she talked about you tonight, woo wee!" He turned towards his truck and walked away shaking his head.

When I got into my own, unacceptable version of a truck, I reached over Alex to get the seatbelt, pulled it across her and secured it without her waking up.

When I got home, I pulled up to the front porch instead of parking in the little garage downstairs. I opened the front door, turned on the light and went back to get her out of the truck, closing the passenger side door with my foot. The sound of the closing door woke her just enough that she wrapped her arms around my neck and slowly mumbled, "Toby."

"I got you." I assured her. She laid her head on my shoulder and fell right back asleep before I walked up the steps and into the house. I closed the front door with my foot, walked around the stone wall through the living room and into the spare bedroom opposite my office. I used the light from the dining room to see and laid her on the bed.

I stood beside the bed for a moment and stared at her considering the right thing to do. I walked into my room, and got a long, button-down shirt out of my closet and went back into the spare room with her.

You have to at least try to wake her up, man. Just leave her alone. She's passed out and won't know any different anyway. What will it be like in the morning if she wakes up and I've helped her get undressed while she's passed out? Shit, there is absolutely no right answer here.

"Alex," I said quietly while touching her shoulder with no response. I raised my voice slightly and shook her a little harder, "Alex." I still got no response. I cleared my throat and shook even harder when I said in a slightly raised tone, "Alex!"

She squinted her eyes in disapproval and then relaxed again. I breathed deeply in through my nose and exhaled strongly out my mouth before starting. I grabbed the bottom of her white shirt in my hands and slowly slid it along her back and up towards her head. When the back of her shirt reached her shoulder blades, I squeezed my hand between her back and the bed to lift her just a little, one shoulder at a time until the back of her shirt was up over her shoulders. I lifted her right hand so that her elbow was bent and pulled her arm through the shirt, exposing her white, satin bra. I walked around the other side of the bed and did the same thing to the left side and her entire shirt was a loose ring around her neck.

Be a gentleman, dumbass. Just make it quick.

Being a gentleman was far easier in my mind than the reality of it, but I did it; as much as possible anyway. I pulled her white shirt up over her head and placed it beside me on the bed. I looked down at her shorts, tightly fitted around her waist.

Just leave them, man. She'll be fine and comfortable just as she is. They're damn near cutting off her circulation. All I have to do is loosen them and leave them on her. Oh, yeah that will certainly be comfortable for her to sleep in. Yeah, right. Just do it, Toby. The more you think about it, the worse this is becoming. Just take care of the lady.

I walked back around the bed again, sighed deeply and unbuckled her belt, unsnapped, then unzipped her jean shorts. That's when I noticed her short boots she was still wearing. I unzipped the sides of the boots, pulled each off and placed them neatly against the wall beside her bed. Without hesitating, I grabbed the bottom of her shorts to pull them down off her hips, then grabbed the waist and slid them off her legs, folded them, put them on top of her boots, then tugged at the sheets from underneath her body and covered her up. I didn't even want to try to put the shirt on her out of fear that she would wake up in the middle of the process. I decided I would rather face her in the morning than in the moment. I lifted her head softly and placed a pillow underneath. She shifted on the bed, turned on her right side, facing me and placed her hand under her face. I left my shirt laying on the bed and walked out of the room, closing the door until there was a thin line of light entering so that she could see if she got up in the middle of the night.

I kept the dining room light on and went into my own room to lay down again. I listened intently to see if I had woken her up but didn't hear any movement from that part of the house. I tried to relax my body and regulate my breathing until it was silent once again. I closed my eyes and felt myself falling asleep but blinked rapidly to stay awake for just a few more moments until I was sure she wouldn't wake up.

I jumped when I heard a loud whisper, "She okay?" from behind me. I rolled over and caught my breath again.

"Yeah, she's okay, she just—wait, how the fuck did you just talk to me?"

"I don't know," I heard in a confused, whispered reply.

"I'm tired and I'm not talking to you any more tonight, Sara. Goodnight."

"Okay, goodnight," she whispered excitedly.

I woke up the next day facing my clock and it was after 10:00. I hadn't slept that late in a long time. That's when I noticed her arm around me. I didn't move for fear of waking her up. She was laying against my back with her arm under my own; our fingers locked together by my chest. I pulled her hand closer and tried to stay relaxed, but my heart began to beat faster.

She shifted, then sighed. I could feel her hot breath between my shoulder blades. I closed my eyes and felt her gently place her mouth in the same place. Chills covered my body. She kissed me again; a sensual kiss that started with her mouth slightly open, then she touched her tongue to my skin and closed her mouth in a kiss. She sighed again and continued kissing up my back. I pulled her hand up to my mouth and kissed it softly. Her kisses reached the pocket between my shoulder and neck and I let out a deep, quiet moan.

"Good morning, Mister Miller," she whispered.

I kissed her hand again and said, "Good morning to you, Miss Reagan. How do you feel?"

"Much better after some sleep and some aspirin a few hours ago."

She kissed again. I turned onto my back and she leaned up on her elbow tracing invisible lines on my chest with the tips of her fingers. I reached my hand around her back and looked into her hazel eyes looking back down at me. I smiled and she smiled back with, "What?"

"It's just that—you're so beautiful."

She smiled bigger and leaned towards me in a deep kiss. What started as lightly caressing each other's skin with our fingertips became firm, passionate rubbing with the full of our hands. I pulled my hand up to her face as we kissed and ran my fingers around her ear and firmly up her scalp, collecting her brunette hair. She rubbed her hand down the front of my leg, then back up the inside. I made a fist with my hand, tightening her hair in my grip when she reached my boxers and took my breath away. She tilted her head back with an open mouth. Both of us were breathing heavily.

"Alex." I said between breaths. "We can't."

"I know," she breathed. "But I want to so badly."

"Me too, baby."

She laid her head on my chest and we tried the best we could to relax. Her skin was soft under my gentle touch. A thought came to mind and I laughed. "You were so drunk last night."

"I know. I never—"

"Yeah, right," I interrupted.

"I swear it, Toby. I just don't put myself in that situation. I have no idea how I got here."

I told her the story of meeting Rick and picking her up from the bench in front of the bar. She was embarrassed but was thankful.

"So, you brought me here, put me in the spare room and took all my clothes off?"

"Not all of them," I said with a grin, then changed the subject. "I figured you'd sleep until noon."

"I woke up around 7:30 and couldn't figure out where I was at first. Once I realized where I was, I was comfortable, so I walked over here to rummage through your medicine cabinet. I felt the headache as soon as I stood up."

"If you got the headache after you were up, what woke you up in the first place?"

"It was weird. I was all covered up with the blankets and that thick comforter, but no matter what I did or how far I pulled the blankets up, I had cold chills all night."

Sara, what are you doing?

Not able to hide the surprised look on my face, Alex asked, "What is it?"

"It's just weird, like you said. Chills; usually alcohol gives a person hot flashes."

"That's what I thought too. It's alright. I'm certainly warm now."

"I am, too, Alex." I kissed her once. "I am, too."

Chapter 14
Details

"I better get myself home. I have a few appointments today," Alex said.

"How exactly are you going to get home when you don't have a vehicle?" I laughed.

"Yeah, I sort of forgot about that."

"Wait, when I picked you up last night, Rick's was the only other vehicle in the parking lot. Where the hell is your car?"

"Oh, he probably hid it around the back of the building. He's been known to do that for a couple of reasons, like when someone's had too much to drink and asks for a ride home, he'll drive the person's car to the back to hide it from passing traffic."

"That's cool." I said.

"Yeah, he's a good guy. The other times he does that is when somebody's too drunk to drive but refuses to take a cab." She began to laugh out loud. "Rick will get the keys from them and hide the car around the back so when their drunk ass goes outside, the car's gone." She laughed harder. "Then these fools walk around the parking lot, all loud, shouting, 'Somebody stole my truck.' It's the funniest thing to watch from inside."

"How the hell does he get the keys from them?"

"Oh, he finds a way. If he can't get them to hand them over, he'll just steal them."

"Should we call just to make sure?"

"No, no need. I'm sure it's there."

She playfully kissed me a few more times and jumped out of the bed. I couldn't help but notice her defined figure in just her bra and underwear as she pranced out of the room. I got dressed and waited in the kitchen for her.

It was only a couple of minutes before she walked out of the spare room with those tight shorts on, the amazing white shirt and the short leather boots. With the keys in my hand, I walked towards the door and said, "Ready?"

She put her arms around me and kissed me again. She looked deep into my eyes and said sensually, "I'm ready whenever you tell me that you are, sugar."

I smiled at her and opened the door to go to the truck. When I closed the door behind me, I jumped down all of the steps to get in front of her to open her door, like a proper gentleman. Only I forgot to unlock the doors, so my hand slipped off the handle and when it didn't open, I stumbled backwards a few steps.

She laughed at me, which was quite appropriate, and I stepped back up to the door, reached into my pocket, pulled out the fob and pushed the unlock button twice. She was still giggling when I held the fob up and said, "Imagine that—keys." I opened her door and offered my hand when she stepped into the truck.

As we drove towards the bar, I asked her, "What was the occasion last night anyway?"

"It's Sara."

My heartbeat raced and I did the best I could to hide my fidgeting. Luckily, Alex was looking out the window and didn't notice me rubbing my hands on the steering wheel nervously.

"What about her?"

"It's been a year. The only time I ever went to Rick's Bar was on our birthday and I wanted to replace the memory of the day she was murdered with something better."

"Part of the process," I said in confirmation

"Yes, exactly."

I thought about making a comment about her saying 'our birthday,' but I didn't. When you keep secrets, sometimes you forget what you're supposed to know and what you're not. I couldn't remember if Alex ever mentioned it or just Sara.

"No comment?" she asked.

"About what?"

"Our birthday?"

"She was your twin," I said casually.

"Yes."

"Do you think that has made it a lot harder on you?"

"Oh, God, yes. Twins have a different relationship; a different bond. In some ways, I think we were tighter than any other siblings we knew. Think about it. Nobody wants to hang out with their little sister or brother. Sara and I were never like that. Neither of us wanted to hang out *without* the other."

"Really?"

"Most of the time, anyway. There were times that I think we fought worse than other siblings too." She started laughing. "One time, we got in a big ol' fight because she wore my shirt without asking. We screamed at each other for a half hour back and forth. We were supposed to be going out together. I don't even remember where we were going. I just remember that we were exhausted from yelling at each other for so long. I walked out of her room and didn't make it ten steps down the hallway and turned back around in tears. I ran into her room, crying, told her how sorry I was and that she could keep the shirt and anything else she wanted of mine."

Her laughter faded, and she stared out the window again completely silent. I reached over to hold her hand.

"Were you alike with everything?"

"Most things, yes, but some things, no. Seraphina was elegant in public; a real lady. People asked all the time why I wasn't more like her. I'd just much rather slam a few beers after working all day in the yard."

"She wouldn't drink beer after working in the yard?"

She laughed hard, "Hell, she never worked in the yard."

"Oh, I see."

"She was always a lady and I've always been more of a—well, I don't know, but I sure as hell have never been ladylike the way she was."

We were approaching Rick's when she said, "I think you would have really liked her."

"It sure sounds like I would have." I pulled into the gravel parking lot. "Now, where did you say that your car should be?"

"Around the back. It looks like the building backs up right to the trees there, but there's a space there."

I drove around the left side of the building where Rick's truck was the night before and saw where she was talking about. I pulled into the small alley and saw her car just as the window passed the building.

"You got your keys on you?" I asked.

She looked in her tiny purse and said, "I sure do. Probably would have been good to check that before we left your place."

I kissed the back of her hand and said, "Yeah, probably."

"You alright, Toby?"

"Yeah, why?"

"You're just not yourself."

I smiled at her and said, "Not sure why, but for some reason, I didn't sleep well last night."

She leaned over and kissed me before she got out and I watched her start the car and put it in Drive. I backed out of the alley and got back on the road, waving out my window when I turned out of the parking lot. She waved back and turned the other direction.

I took a deep breath and sighed heavily as I depressed the gas pedal a little more. I sped back left and right navigating the bends in the road, trying to get back home. I had to try to figure out how Sara spoke to me without any equipment.

When I got home, I pulled up to the front of the house and ran inside, yelling, "Sara," like a father yelling for a lost child.

"Sara, where are you?"

I stood in the middle of the living room so that I could hear her from any area of the house.

"Sara."

The hair on my arm stood up when I felt her touch my arm, and she replied with, "I'm right here."

"How are you able to talk?"

"I really don't know."

"Will I be able to see you someday?"

"Yeah, I don't know that either," she said snidely.

"Wow, your sister just told me that you were not so much alike, but I'm not sure I believe it." I said with a smile. There was silence for a while. "Did you leave?"

"No, I'm right here at the table."

"Okay then. The table, it is." I sat down and said, "Ah, where should I start?"

"Oh, no, sir. That's not how this is going to work today. You *drilled* me with questions last night."

I felt like I was getting scolded, so I pulled a chair out and sat down. "What do you have in mind, Sara?"

She laughed and said, "It's my turn. I'll be asking the questions today."

"Yes, ma'am. Um, do you mind if I get a drink first?"

"It's your house now; do as you please."

"Is it now? Is this really my house? I'm only here because you're —because you—"

"Because I'm dead?"

I dropped my shoulders in shame and said, "Yes."

"Why don't you go get that drink."

"Yes, ma'am," I said and stood up from the table to walk into the kitchen. I made my drink and sat it on the table on top of a coaster. I didn't want to feel so lonely, so I went back and made another one and set it at her place on the table.

"Thank you," she said. "What exactly am I going to do with this?"

"It's for my own sanity, Sara." I sipped my drink and leaned back in my chair. "Where do we begin?"

"What are your intentions with my sister?"

"Wow, not one for easing into it, are you?"

"No."

"My intention is to not build a wall around me. I don't want to be guarded. I want to live my life, as I promised Anna."

"So, you're interested in my sister because of a promise made to your wife?"

"No, that's not it at all." I knew immediately that she wasn't just asking casual questions. The questioning was worse than if I were talking to their father to obtain his acceptance.

I took another drink and said seriously, "Look, my intention is to not hide my feelings for anyone, ever. And yes, it's because of Anna. Not *for* Anna, but *because* of her. What I would give for the chance to tell her I love her one more time. I made a deal with Alex. She's devastated over losing you, so we're both learning to live again— together."

"Anna was your whole world, wasn't she?"

"Of course, she was. We did everything together, not because we felt as though we had to, but because we wanted to. We had a unique love that people couldn't understand. We didn't fight, we never raised our voices at each other, and we respected each other. Don't get me wrong, we disagreed sometimes. Plenty of times, really. The difference is that we disagreed with each other respectfully. We each had an opinion and were genuinely interested in the other's without trying to change it. We took every potential 'you're wrong' situation and turned it into learning what the other thinks, believes and dreams. Ultimately, it became the culture of our marriage."

"So much love, it's hard to believe it was real."

"We heard that a lot," I said.

"I wish I would have recognized how awful Daryl was to me."

"Sara, you can't blame yourself for that."

"Why not? Everybody else saw it. Everyone but me. I just thought he loved me. I thought we were soulmates because we had so many things in common. The same music, the same background, the same religion. We watched the same movies, agreed on most controversial issues in the world—I could go on and on. Did I recognize that something had gotten a little weird? Of course, I did. It just didn't feel right, but I ignored my own emotions and talked myself into believing that we were actually getting closer."

"Think of it this way, Sara, you certainly got rid of him."

"I'm just glad I had the chance to watch the son of a bitch die before me."

I mixed another drink and stood in the kitchen. "I'm going to have to get an old picture of you or something to put at your spot at the table. I feel weird talking into the air."

"You've done fine looking at me."

"I just wish I could see you when we talk. You can see me."

"Yes, I can, and I've seen a lot of you," she laughed.

"Here's a question for you, if you don't mind." I said.

"Sure, anything."

"The night you died, you were standing here in the kitchen?"

"Yes."

"And he was somewhere over there." I pointed through the galley kitchen. "He was yelling at you."

"Yes," she said more seriously; almost sternly.

"He fired, and you dropped to the floor right here." I stood over to the corner. "You opened the corner cabinet to get the pistol out and shot him, and he was right about here." I walked to the edge of the galley kitchen.

"What are you getting at, Toby?"

"Now that I play it out again, I think I have two questions." I stood back at the edge of the kitchen bar and looked back and forth at the places where each of them laid that night. I stopped when I looked into the corner where Sara died. "Why did you stay behind?"

She began to cry and said, "I stayed for Alex. I needed her to know how sorry I was that I didn't see the signs before. I needed her to really understand that it wasn't her fault. She always tried to blame herself for anything bad that happened to me, and I didn't want her to live like that."

"Yet, you've never tried to contact her to tell her?"

The glass I set in front of her began to move towards the edge of the table, just a little at a time.

"No," she said, no longer crying.

"It just seems odd to me that you're stuck here in this house because of a decision you made to stay behind. You made that decision to make sure your sister is at peace and you've never told her."

The glass moved a little more and began to tilt to one side, making the contents slosh around like an angry sea.

"Toby, why is this important to you?"

"I'm just trying to understand. That's all."

"Why?"

"No, Sara, I don't think so. You've asked enough questions for today. It's my turn again. Alex told me every detail of what happened that night and you just confirmed the story, so I wonder how she knows every detail when she only heard it through the phone?"

Her glass launched across the room and broke on the big wall next to the spare room door. With my heart beating fast, I walked over to pick the pieces off the floor. I heard her crying again. I stood up holding the pieces of glass in my hand and turned around.

I was more surprised than ever, "Oh, my God. Sara?"

Chapter 15

Pieces

I ran over to sit next to her, but she vanished as quickly as she appeared. Her hair was long, straight and flowing over her right shoulder. She was hiding her sobbing face in her hands and I could still hear her crying. I put the broken glass on the table.

"Sara, I'm so sorry. I won't bring it up again. I never meant to upset you, I just wanted to understand."

I knelt down next to her chair and reached out to touch her but felt nothing. I curved my hand around where her face should be and said, "Sara, use my energy to show yourself again—please."

I felt her cold touch gently on the side of my face and she finally spoke through sobs, "Please, Toby, stop asking questions. I beg you, please."

"I'm sorry, sweetheart, really. I'm so sorry."

In an instant, I couldn't hear her anymore. The entire house fell into silence. I couldn't feel her presence at all. She was gone.

I walked around the house calling her name but got no response. When I got back to the dining room, I tried one last time. Without a response, I looked around a, once again, silent house. I walked over to the table and finished the rest of my beverage, then put the glass in the kitchen and leaned on the bar counter staring out at—nothing.

It was only mid-afternoon and the day was bright. I walked around to turn off all of the electronics, but the silence was driving me crazy. I hadn't been in the house a full week, and other than Saturday, my first full day in the house, there was someone here with me, be it Alex or Sara, I had someone to talk to. I was alone again, trying to determine how to keep myself busy. I took notice of the empty walls, opened all the doors and windows again, then set the framed prints in different places on the floor, leaning up against the wall. Before hanging any of them, I broke the silence with the radio. I kept the volume low in case Sara returned and wanted to talk.

Hanging pictures was a slow process because my mind kept going back to Sara, then to Alex and back to Sara. I never meant to hurt her and didn't know exactly why my questions affected her so much. The only thing I was confident about was that I didn't know the truth about what happened the night Sara and Daryl died.

I spent the afternoon hanging photographs in every room and fine-tuning things around the house. The last thing I did was vacuum the floor; not because it was particularly dirty, but because with all the movement, I couldn't see the vacuum cleaner lines anymore. As every man knows, as long as there are vacuum cleaner lines, there is a clean house.

I got a beer and sat on the back porch to watch the sunset. It was a perfect night to sit in the mountain air. The breeze was light and the sun cast a glow from just behind the distant mountain. The chirping birds faded out one by one until only a few distinct birdsongs remained. I heard sticks snap in the woods in front of me that seemed to be coming from the trail back to the gazebo. I scanned the tree line several times when the source became visible. As graceful as a cat, a large black bear walked out of the woods at an angle towards the back of the garage. She looked in all directions as she walked, then suddenly stopped when she noticed me. I stared at her and she stared right back at me. She turned her head towards the tree line where she just came from and nodded her head up and down dramatically, as if communicating. She turned back to me again and slowly continued her path.

I was in awe with a smile stretched broadly across my face when I saw them. One, two, three bear cubs came out of the woods behind her in a single file line, leaping to catch up with their momma. The militant style didn't last long. The smallest one in the back veered off to the left, ran around the other two and up to Momma. When the other two caught up with him, the littlest ran off on his own again, circling the others. That didn't please Momma. She stopped in an instant, turned around, lifted her front left paw and pounded it once on the ground with a low thud. Without another warning, all three lined up again perfectly behind her and disappeared into the tree line to my right.

I heard the hot tub motor come on and went into the enclosure to check the chemicals. I added a scoop of chlorine and left the lid open after I turned on the jets for a cycle. I walked inside through the bedroom and into the kitchen. I leaned up against the cabinet closest to the front door and imagined each event unfold as I replayed the account in my mind.

She was abused—He didn't know I came over so much—He didn't allow it—The more you try to make them believe, the more they pull away —who the fuck are you talking to now—NO—that useless fucking sister of yours—that's when I heard the gunshot.

It was a believable story and I would have never questioned it, had Sara not reacted the way she did. I believed there was something missing that was purposely omitted from Alex's story and didn't dismiss the possibility that part of it was a lie.

I went into the office and searched the internet for anything regarding the deaths on May 6 of the previous year. I came across Sara's obituary. There was no picture, there wasn't much information and her last name that was published was strange to me.

"Reagan. Weird. Let's see here, Sara Reagan was taken into God's hands unexpectedly on May 6. Sara is survived by her sister. This is the strangest obit I think I've ever read. No full name, no age, no cause of death, no mention of being married and certainly no listings for Daryl at all."

I checked the websites for many of the local papers around the same publication date and none of them had a listing for Daryl. I looked on social media sites. There was no listing for Alex, Sara or Daryl. I texted Alex.

> Hey there. I was trying to find
> you on social media and can't.
> Do you have a site?

I watched the dots until the message appeared.

> Hey sweetie, you won't find me
> on social media. I don't do that
> shit. I'm a very private person
> and have no interest in telling
> people everything about me,

from my beliefs to when I
started LOL.

I put my phone down on the desk and unlocked my computer screen. "Damn, that's a hell of a shot," I said out loud when I saw the image I was editing when Alex arrived that day in the rain. I saved it and scanned through some of the others I took, trying to decide on which one I would work on next.

The bustle of the previous days and the broken sleep the night before had me in bed before it was completely dark. I laid in bed thinking of May 6, trying to put it all together so that I could understand the whole story, at the same time, I also knew that there were pieces missing.

I rolled over on my left side and gently touched the pillow. There were no eyes smiling back at me and no blonde hair cascading over the pillow. I turned over on my right side and tried to think of Alex but couldn't envision her lying next to me. I lifted my head and looked through the French doors into the kitchen hoping to hear or see a glimpse of Sara, but she was still gone. I slid my boxers off from under the covers and threw them in the corner, hoping they would at least land *close* to the laundry basket. My eyes got heavier so I settled into my pillow to sleep.

The next morning when I woke, I got a cup of coffee before putting on any clothing at all and opened the front door. I stuck my head out and looked all around to be certain there were no houses visible, then stepped out over the threshold and looked around again. When I felt comfortable enough, I walked over to the wooden rocking chair closest to the door on my left, carefully rubbed my fingers across it for splinters and sat down. I rocked slowly back and forth, sipping my coffee and enjoying the sights and sounds of nature—completely naked. I drank the full cup of coffee then went inside to get more.

I thought a lot about Alex. Not about the story she told me, but the story we were making together. I still couldn't describe the connection, nor did I lose any sleep trying to understand it. Part of learning how to live again had to include living life and not always trying to understand it. A song entered my mind and I went down to the basement to play it on my drum set. Wearing nothing but the drumsticks in my hand, I scrolled through my music player and found "There's No One Like You" from The Scorpions. I played through that song and continued as I usually did; with over 2,000 songs in my library ranging across multiple genres, I tried to play along with anything that randomly started playing. I didn't have an expectation of myself to play it perfectly, but simply play along. There weren't many full songs that I knew how to play well; just pieces of them, then picked up a beat that matched and hoped for the best.

I had barely left the house since I moved in and I wanted to get out. I knew I was going out with Alex on Friday night and I also knew I hadn't finished putting together the photographs from my last day out. I had also started writing the book but couldn't get beyond writing the part about being woken up by Amy the morning Anna died.

I looked at the weather app on my phone and it was supposed to be sunny all day, with a high of seventy-two. Most people would say that's a perfect situation for a day in the park, but as a landscape photographer, the sun was my enemy based on the photos I tried to capture.

I had to focus on something. Anything that I could start and finish. My life was spread all over. Not only the house, the photographs, and the book, but my emotions were, too. A piece of me was still holding on to Anna, afraid to go into the park where her memory was scattered everywhere I looked. Another piece of me was trying to start a relationship with Alex; something I hadn't done in over fourteen years. There was a piece that was intrigued, if not bordering obsessed, with Sara. Still, another piece of me was trying to live normally by taking photographs in the park and selling them on my website, which was, admittedly, a strategy for moving on. It's the one thing I knew I did well.

I got dressed, made some toast and another cup of coffee, then went into the office to finalize the other photographs and got completely lost in my work. I inspected photo after photo to ensure I captured exactly the right setting, colors, saturation, depth of field, vibrancy, and cleanliness after editing. I chose one of them to be my desktop background for a week, so I could look at it over and over to see if anything else needed to be cleaned up. If I was still pleased after a week, I'd post it to my photography site. That was the process I went through with every photo I took.

"Toby."

"Sara," I responded instantly. "Where are you and where have you been?"

"It's the strangest feeling. I get really weak sometimes. I think it's tied to my emotions."

"Weak, in what way?"

"I compare it to being tired when I was alive. Not just sleepy, but it's like the feeling you get when your whole body needs to shut down and you just can't do any more."

"And you feel normal now?"

"No, I just needed to talk to you and apologize for the way I acted yesterday."

"Sara, where are you?"

"I'm here, right beside you, as always."

I smiled at her and she laughed lightly right next to me. "Shall we sit?" I asked.

"Of course, but why don't you get comfortable and sit on the couch instead of at the table?"

I did as she recommended and opened the recliner on the end of the couch. It was awkward when she didn't speak for a few moments. "Sara?"

"I'm here," I heard her right next to me again, but she was much closer this time. Her voice seemed louder, but she also spoke softer, like she was speaking right into my ear. I felt the, now familiar, cold sensation on the side of my face and jumped.

"Don't," she said. "I need to learn more about being this way. Will you help me?"

"How could I ever teach you anything about it?"

"You can start by leaning back."

I pushed the recliner out with my feet so that I was laying back farther and asked anxiously, "What are you trying to learn?"

"I want to know how you feel me. If I can change what I do to make you feel me differently, maybe it won't be so cold."

"Okay, what do you want me to do?"

"Just tell me what you feel—you have to relax, Toby."

"Forgive me, but it's a little hard to relax. You're asking me to trust you without really knowing what you're going to do. Besides, it sounds a little—you know—personal."

"Tobias," she said elegantly. "I will never hurt you. I just want you to tell me what you feel."

I followed her instructions.

"Take a few deep breaths and relax. Really focus on relaxing."

I was still tense, and she knew it. She said, "Here, I'm going to put my hand on your arm first."

"Okay—phew, that's cold."

"Does it hurt?"

"No, just cold. Wait, it's really just a surprising feeling. I'm getting used to it now. It's still cold, but not—whatever. It's hard to explain."

"I'm going to lift my hand and put it on your other arm."

"I feel it, but it's not so bad. Maybe because I expected it."

"Good," she whispered. "Now, can you relax a little more?"

"I'll try. Wait, what are your intentions here?" I said as I sat up just a little.

She didn't reply. I leaned back again and tried to relax.

She finally spoke, "If you're ready—"

I took a deep breath and tried to relax all at once.

I couldn't see or hear anything, but my other senses kicked in and I felt amazing, although I wouldn't admit that to Sara. It was like being blindfolded and anxiously anticipating what was going to happen next. I explained what I felt as soon as she began again.

"I feel you touching my head. It's cold, but not too cold—you're touching the side of my face on the left side—now my right—hmm, this kinda feels nice. You're rubbing your finger down my chest; then back up each side again. I can feel you on the outside of my arm—now the other arm—okay, now this seems odd. I feel cold—on both sides of my face."

She whispered, "Open your eyes."

I opened them and was looking directly into hazel eyes, not two inches away from my face. She leaned closer and touched her lips to mine.

"Mmm, Ale—" I stopped before I finished the name. I pushed my head backwards in the chair cushion when the realization hit me; this wasn't Alex. It was her sister. I opened my eyes and, without wanting to bring more attention to the awkward situation, I just explained what I felt.

"I only feel the cold sensation, Sara. I can't feel your lips at all—what do you feel?"

"Nothing."

"Nothing?" I asked surprised.

"No, not anything at all." There was slight frustration in her tone as she stood up and walked around the living room. "I can smell you. I smell your cologne all the time. I can see you. I've watched you for the last week. I watched you when Alex brought you inside. I watch you sleep. I watch you walk around the house. I watch you when you're working. I can hear you. I hear you laugh, I hear you cry. I hear you talk to Anna. I hear the love you had for her. I hear how amazing you are to my sister. I see you everywhere, Toby, even when you're gone, and I can hear you when you're not home. I can touch you, but I can't feel you. I can kiss you, but I can't taste you. There are pieces of you that I want so badly; the rest, I only long for because I can't have it."

She sat next to me again, "I would give anything to be able to taste you and to feel you—but I have nothing to give."

I reached out to touch her face, but only felt the cold on the palm of my hand. "Oh, Sara, I can't imagine what that's like for you."

I smiled and said, "Do you have any idea how fucked up this is? I'm taking your sister out on a date tomorrow night and you're confessing feelings for me. Sara, you're not even—"

"I know. Like I said before, I have nothing to offer you. You have so much love; love like I've never had."

"I wish you could be at peace with that. I mean—"

"I was," she interrupted. "Until you showed up."

"Do I need to keep Alex away from here? Does it bother you that she and I are—whatever we are?"

Her visible presence began to fade again.

"Please don't. I have to see my sister."

"Okay, but you know, the other morning, we—"

"I know. When she went into your room, I went downstairs. I'll stay away whenever she's here when you need time alone."

"I think she deserves to know you're here," I told her.

"Why?"

"I'm not comfortable with a secret like that. I'm going to tell her."

"Toby, please; let me."

"Okay, I won't say anything, but don't wait too long or I will."

With that, she was gone again. I was curious and, admittedly, a little nervous about how Sara was going to let Alex know of her presence. I had seen first-hand that when she got emotional, things got broken. I spent more time alone before Friday evening came and didn't hear or see any hint of Sara, but that didn't mean she wasn't in my thoughts. It was ironic that I was learning to live again, and she was learning about death. I was her test subject and her first experiment was one of the most sensual experiences of my life; an experience I had to dismiss.

Chapter 16

Exposed

I tried hard to focus on my date with Alex. I felt completely out of my league in a game I didn't even know how to play anymore. Nevertheless, I wanted to impress her, and it didn't take long until every thought I had was how to do that very thing.

I looked around the house with a different set of eyes, looking as a visitor instead of a widowed man with lower standards for cleanliness and décor. The framed prints certainly made it feel more like a home. It was more like the forever house that Anna and I dreamed of than it had ever been. I spent the rest of that day and the next morning mounting televisions on the wall and hiding cords. Early Friday afternoon, I went to buy some scented candles for the house and eight taper candles for the sconces on the gazebo. I still didn't have a solid plan as to where to take her or what we were going to do. Certainly, nothing I would come up with at the last minute would impress her, like I had hoped.

The previous two days seemed like an eternity, but leading up to 6:00, it felt like the clock just decided to skip every other hour.

6:00. 6:00. Really, 6:00? Why couldn't I make it 7:00? Maybe I did say 7:00. Dammit, I don't remember. I know I said Friday night and I know I said I'd pick her up, but I don't think I said a time.

I pulled out my phone and sent a text

Hi Alex

Hi Toby. You're killing me here.
The anticipation is driving me
crazy.   What time are you
coming to pick me up?

Really? I thought to myself. I laughed out loud about the fact that she believed I was building her anticipation when, in reality, I hadn't even thought of a time.

7:00.

And what are we going to do?

You'll have to get used to
anticipation, my dear. I want to
surprise you.

You're an ass, Tobias.

LOL. See you soon.

I took one last look around the house. It was as ready as it was ever going to be. I did the best I could to come up with plans for the night while I was in the shower.

Deciding what to wear was more stressful than the previous two days. I didn't want to dress too nicely but didn't want to look like a bum. I decided on fitted dark jeans, with black socks, dress shoes and a white dress shirt with a button-down collar. Just before I left at 6:30, I got a text from Alex with her address that started with, "Unless you're some sort of stalker and already have it, here's my address." I simply replied with, "Thank you, Miss Reagan."

The GPS took me right to it. She lived in a modern house in a very nice neighborhood. I parked in the driveway and was completely lost again.

"Do I go ring the doorbell? Do I stay out here and honk the horn?

I laughed out loud at the thought.

It's 7 minutes till 7. Dammit, just go in. "

I turned off the truck and walked up to ring the bell, but she opened the door as I reached for it. She greeted me while hopping on one foot to get her boot on. When her foot sank into the shoe, she leaned her head to the side with her hair over her shoulder, trying to put an earring in the other side.

"Wow, I'm impressed," I told her. "can you do that with your eyes closed too?"

She laughed and invited me in. She closed the door behind me as she finally got her foot into the shoe and said, "I probably can, want to see?"

We both laughed and she ran up the stairs directly across from the front door shouting behind her, "I'll be ready in just a couple minutes."

She was wearing tight, light blue jeans with a powder blue shirt that fell off her shoulders and, after the acrobatic greeting, two short boots.

"It's okay, I'm a little early."

I looked around the house. There was a place for everything. It was all decorated so perfectly. Through the sitting room on the right, there was a fireplace on the outside wall. Above it, a large, studio print of her and Sara hung against the stone. I heard drawers open and close upstairs and her footsteps darting from room to room above me.

"Ha!" she shouted from upstairs excitedly. "I found it." She stopped at the top of the stairs and turned around quickly as though she had forgotten something. She walked into a doorway and I heard a cabinet door open, four or five sprays and the cabinet door close again. She sighed at the top of the steps and walked down slowly with a smile. When she reached the bottom, she held up a silver necklace, handed it to me and said, "Do you mind helping me with this?"

I made sure I had the clasp in my right hand and she turned her back to me. I stretched my arms out in front of her and she put both of her hands up under the back of her hair and lifted, revealing her neck to me again. I bit my lip and secured the necklace just before she let her hair down again and shook it back and forth. She turned around, fidgeting with the charm on the end of the necklace and asked, "Is it okay?"

I put my hand on hers which made her let go of the necklace and she dropped her shoulders in a relieving sigh.

"It's perfect," I said as I looked into her eyes.

She walked around once, turned on a couple of lights and got her wallet off the stand by the front door when she made a full circle.

I put my hand on the small of her back, kissed her gently and asked, "Ready?" with a smile.

"Ready," she confirmed.

I opened her door for her when we reached the SUV and reached out my hand. She took it with a smile and sat down before letting go. When she lifted her legs in, I closed the door and walked around the front to get to the other side.

"Where you takin' me, Mr. Miller?"

I spoke like a butler, "The evening will start at my place. There's a bottle of wine chilling on the counter and—"

Her laughter made me laugh at myself.

"And what, Mr. Miller?"

I stopped laughing, and broke character when I said, "Alex, the truth is, I have no fucking clue."

She laughed so hard, she rocked back and forth in the seat and pulled her legs up off the floor. I tried to keep control of my own laughter, so I could drive right, but the more I tried not to laugh, the more tears came down my face.

"Are you serious, Toby?"

"Yes ma'am, I'm afraid I am," I said more seriously, but still smiling.

She reached over to hold my hand, turned towards me and said, "I think it's perfect."

"Good. I'm glad you think so,"

I could see out of the corner of my eye that she was smiling at me. I smiled back, pulled her hand up to kiss it and said, "because there's no wine chilling either," which made her laugh all over again.

When we got back to my place, I parked in the front and ran over to her side to open her door for her. She took my hand and we walked up the steps to the porch.

Panicked, my heart began to race as soon as I opened the door. I saw candles lit all around the house with soft music playing; but it wasn't my house. I saw the couch and love seat in an L. There was a white tablecloth in a diamond shape on the square coffee table. The gas fireplace was lit, and a fondue pot warmed the chocolate in the middle of the table surrounded by dessert snacks for dipping.

Anna's voice faded into Alex's when she said, "Oh, my God, Toby, it's perfect."

I put my hands on the counter and looked around the house. My house. The forever house with the kitchen to the left, the galley kitchen to the right and the dining room right in front of me. I stepped forward and looked into the living room on the other side of the stone wall. I glanced over at Alex as she was still looking around in awe. I took a deep breath and said in as normal of a tone as I could, "So, you like it?"

"Of course, I do." I conjured a smile just as she looked over to me and said, "I love it. The pictures are so good. If I stand close enough to them, it's like I'm right there."

She noticed the jar candles set in several places and took the top off of each new scent to smell it. "Wow, what else did you do?"

"Feel free to look around anywhere you'd like," I said.

She did, and I walked around the kitchen counter to go to the master bathroom, ensuring I had some additional time to compose myself after my imagination force-fed me a strong dose of the past. I heard cabinets opening from the kitchen, then a bottle clang on the granite countertop. The refrigerator opened and then I heard the distinct sound of a can opening. The radio came on and I heard her yell, "I hope you don't mind if I make myself a drink."

I smiled into the mirror as confirmation to myself that all was okay and yelled back through the closed door, "Of course not. Make yourself at home," before going back to the kitchen.

She was standing in front of a large canvas print of the back side of an old mill. It was pouring the day I took the picture. I had stopped at that spot every time I visited and was never completely satisfied with the outcome until I took the one she was standing in front of.

She took a sip from her glass, then said, "Reagan's Mill."

"Yes, on the Motor Nature Trail. Wait—Reagan—are you related somehow?"

"Of course, I am. Didn't you know we're all related down here?" She laughed and continued seriously, "My last name is just as common as Ogle and Tipton around these parts. I assume we're all related to those people somehow but can't tell you exactly how." She turned back to the photograph. "This print is fascinating. The more I look into it, the deeper it becomes, with the mist in the background and the cascading water. It's really beautiful, Toby."

"Thank you."

She walked around from picture to picture staring into each one of them, slowly swaying her hips to the music as if one part of her was trapped inside the photograph and another part was lost in the music.

She stopped at the cabinet, pointed at one picture, turned to me and asked, "Anna?"

"Yes."

She picked it up and looked at it for a while. "She was beautiful."

I walked up next to her and looked at the picture with her. In a soft voice, she said, "Wow, Toby, you two were so happy."

"Yes, we were," I said with a smile. "You getting hungry at all?"

"I'm starting to, yes."

"What sounds good?"

She sipped her beverage and kept the glass up to her mouth while thinking, then blurted out, "Pizza."

"Pizza? Really? Is there a decent pizza place I can take you?"

She walked over to me, put one of her arms around me and said, "Yes, I know a wonderful place not far away."

I smiled back at her and said, "You do now?"

"Yep. Sure do."

"Where is it?"

She stepped backwards, outstretched her arms and said, "Right here, Tobias." She spun around once to the music. "Right here."

"I'm always good with ordering in. Tell me a good place to order from."

"Rick's has a good pizza and they deliver."

It was decided. Pizza at home was how we were going to spend our time together on our very first date. She called it in since she knew the people there, then insisted that I show her around the house at all the other things I had done, which wasn't much, but I gave her the best tour I could. The evening was perfect. We listened to music, danced around the house, sang along to popular songs and enjoyed our gourmet delivery in a box.

After a while, we went out to the enclosed patio and sat in the rocking chairs in front of the fireplace with our drinks. We shared stories of childhood, previous relationships and anything else we could think of to talk about.

A chill filled the air as we rocked with our fingers joined over the small table between the chairs. She pulled her feet up onto the chair to maintain her body heat. I only had a few pieces of wood but lit a fire in the fireplace to keep us warm. The music played quietly through the outdoor speakers. The fire warmed us on the outside while the liquor kept us warm on the inside. Out of the corner of my eye, I noticed her looking over at me. I turned to her and smiled as the reflection of the fire danced in her hair and highlighted every perfect curve of her face. She stood up slowly, never letting go of my hand or her glass. When she got directly in front of me, she pulled my hand lightly as a subtle request to stand up. When I did, we leaned into each other and kissed softly.

"Thank you," she said.

"For what?"

"An almost perfect night."

"*Almost* perfect?" I asked.

She smiled broadly and led me through the sliding door into the master bedroom. We undressed each other slowly and sensually. With the blinds open, the fire cast a flickering amber glow into the room, making the romantic setting even more perfect than it already was. We explored each other's bodies purposefully; an erotic ending to a perfect evening.

I woke up with the sunrise on that cool morning, made a pot of coffee and went to the patio to rekindle the fire and rocked back and forth in my flannel pants. The sun was coming up to my left, but the light hadn't cast shadows on the Tennessee mountains yet. I heard the door slide open and turned to look as she walked out wearing my white button-down shirt that extended down to the middle of her thighs and a cup of coffee for herself. She stood directly in front of me, as she did the night before, sipped her coffee with a smile and set it on the little table. She turned her body sideways and sat in the rocking chair with me, laying her head on my shoulder and said, "Good morning, Mr. Miller."

"Good morning to you, Miss Reagan."

I rubbed her arm with my left hand and her leg with my right, occasionally reaching to take another drink of coffee. When I set my cup down, she began to kiss my neck. I put my hand on the side of her face and we kissed until I picked her up and carried her back through the sliding glass door once again.

We laid on our backs, side by side, catching our breath. That's when everything changed. She took a deep breath and stayed perfectly still. I looked over at her with a puzzled look, trying to stay as quiet as possible.

"Do you hear that?" she said.

"Barely, but yes."

Our eyes darted back and forth in confusion as we listened.

"What it is?" I asked.

Her eyes opened wide and she let out a terrifying scream with tears instantly falling from her eyes. She stood up and put the white shirt back on, screaming, "SARA—SARA, WHERE ARE YOU?" while she ran through the house and the unmistakable final notes played from a mysteriously sinister jack-in-the-box somewhere in the house.

Chapter 17

The Ghost Between Us

I jumped out of bed and ran after her, "Alex, what's going on?"

She was hysterical when I found her in the spare bedroom sitting on the bed. I sat next to her gently, pulled her arms to me and said, "Come here, baby. Come here."

She put her head into my shoulder and gasped for air as she cried.

"Honey, it's okay. Try to take deep breaths." I held her close to me with one hand and my other stroked her hair. She finally regulated her breathing after several minutes, at the same time, I noticed the plastic clown face extended from the colorful box on the nightstand with a tiny crank on the side.

"Alex, what is that?"

She pulled away from me but didn't look at me or respond.

"Sweetheart, what is it?"

She sighed. "That was mine when I was little. I loved it. I cranked that box and watched that clown pop out ten times a day, it seemed. I laughed and laughed. It terrified Sara, particularly as we got older and the notes didn't play as clearly as they did when it was new. She said it belonged in—"

She stopped talking completely and looked around the room.

"It belonged in what, sweetheart?"

She looked at me expressionless and said, "In a haunted house."

I put my hands on her arms. "Alex, it's okay."

Her look became a punishing glare and she slowly said, "You know— she's here, isn't she? You knew it and you didn't tell me."

"I wanted to, Alex. I wanted to so badly, but I didn't feel as though it was my place to say something." Her eyes squinted in disgust and focused directly into mine, alternating from one eye to the other and I continued, "She said she wanted to be the one to tell you."

"Oh, my God, Toby, she talks to you?" she said angrily.

"We've met."

She put both of her hands in front of me in a gesture telling me to get back. I reached for her hands with mine and said, "I'm so sorry, Alex." As soon as my fingers brushed her hands, she pulled them away, "Don't touch me," she said as she stood up and put her hands on her head. I stood up and she briskly walked through the living room and through the French doors. By the time I reached the doorway, she was already starting to get dressed.

"Alex, please; can we talk about this?"

"Just take me home, Toby."

I started to ask again, but decided it was best to get myself dressed and respect her request. As I stepped into my jeans, I heard the front door open then close hard. I sat on the bed to put my shoes on and looked around the room while I tied them.

"Sara, what have you done?" I whispered.

I went into the kitchen, got my keys off the counter and walked out the door. As soon as I stepped out, Alex stepped off the porch and stood by the door of the truck. When I unlocked it, she opened the door and got in immediately. Nothing was said during the entire drive to her house by either one of us. As I came to a stop in front of her house, I said, "Alex, can we please—" but she got out of the truck without saying a word before I could finish. She ran into her house and closed the door behind her. With both hands on the steering wheel, I dropped my head with a sigh, then pulled away slowly.

When I got home, I parked the truck in the little garage and put my keys on the counter when I got to the kitchen. I looked through the French doors at the white button-down shirt strewn across the bed, with a fresh reminder of how things in life change so quickly.

I walked out to the covered patio to check the fire that had become little more than glowing logs. I sat in the rocking chair, caught in a trance of the dancing flames and replayed the recent times I spent with Alex. She had become part of my life; a part I couldn't easily let go of. I've always believed that the person I am is a combination of every person who's ever influenced my life. When I was younger, I tried hard not to let people in until the person I kept out the most told me of her upcoming marriage. I was devastated because I loved her so much. I swore to myself that day I would never again suppress my feelings for anyone, which came with a cost. I pay with a frequent broken heart. I loved Anna early, but I didn't believe I was good enough for her. She healed every broken piece of my heart when she made me believe that I was.

I got close to Alex quickly. Some would say it was far too quickly, but I disagree. Time doesn't dictate feelings, only the heart can do that. I had let her in and she became a part of me. Sure, my heart was broken again, but my life was altered because of her. Once I let someone in, a piece of them becomes part of me forever.

I went to the office and unlocked the computer to capture my thoughts that morning in the only way I could.

"A Frozen Moment"

I think about you a little
Is every second of the day too much?
I think about the gazebo
That's the first time that we touched.

That frozen moment in time
Our faces an inch apart
A minute later we smiled
And that's where all this starts.

A million thoughts inside our heads
We couldn't begin to sort them out.
On the swing, good things were confirmed,
Now, days later, I'm filled with doubt.

We found something in each other
That we both had found before.
"You'll know it when it happens."
Well, it happened, and we wanted more.

But changes in this life
Keep the future just a mystery.
So, until we find a way,
Our frozen moment is simply history.

　　　　　　　　　　　　　　~Tobias Miller

I turned off my computer, showered and laid back down. The activities the previous night, although incredible, had me awake more than I slept. I wondered if I should contact Alex again and, if so, when. I also thought of what I would say to her. *Should I text? Should I give it a couple of days and call?* I reached for my phone on the belt clip of my jeans on the floor next to the bed and sent one last message.

> I'm sorry as hell for keeping such a secret. If and when I could ever be given a chance to rebuild your trust, I'll be here.

I was notified that she had read it within seconds, but she didn't respond. I flipped the switch on the side of the phone so it was no longer on mute, like I kept it most of the time, and set the phone on the nightstand next to me. I grabbed the white shirt and held it up to my nose. I could smell her and that was comforting.

I woke up a couple of hours later and immediately looked at my phone hoping I would have a response. Nothing. I stared at the ceiling with my hands folded under my head for a while before getting up and finding things to do to keep my mind occupied. I went back into the office and sat at the computer, but without being able to focus on anything, the screen saver came back on before I started anything. I walked around the house, looking at the pictures on the walls, then looked into the different rooms searching for a hint of a spotlight, an actor or a guest in my cold, dark theater, but there was none. I stood by the sliding glass door and looked at the sunny backyard, but the light couldn't penetrate the emptiness I felt inside.

"Toby."

I sighed without looking away from the backyard. "What do you want, Sara?"

"I'm sorry. I thought that would work."

I never raised my voice when I turned around and saw her sitting at the table, "Now, how in the fuck did you ever think that would work, Sara? Play an old, out of tune jack-in-the-box? The creepiest toy ever made?"

"It was hers and I hated it, but—"

"I know about it. Did you not hear her explain it to me just before she made me take her home?"

"No, I stayed away this time until I went to the attic to get the toy. I truly am sorry, Toby."

I sat at the table across from her. Perhaps it was because she was Alex's twin, but it was difficult to stay too angry. "It's my fault. I should have told her myself the first time I spoke to you through the spirit box." I wanted to offer her a forgiving smile but couldn't allow it.

"What are we going to do now?" she asked.

"I don't know, but I'm not sure I trust your ideas. Let's just give her some time, okay?"

"Okay. We can do that." We both remained silent for a minute until she asked, "So, how did it go?"

I thought about my date and smiled, "It was amazing, Sara. All of it. From boxed pizza to dancing to—" I thought of our activities that kept us up most of the night and decided not to share that part. "Everything right up until you cranked that jack-in-the-box."

I looked over at her, but she had her head down and didn't notice. "Has she ever done something like this before; just walk out when she's mad?"

"Oh yes, all the time. Not ever because of a man that I can remember, but it's how she copes. She just goes into hiding for a few days and will come out with a clear mind."

"Maybe that's what I should do, just stay here for a while until my mind is clear."

She looked up at me and said, "Do you want me to leave?"

I considered it for some time, comparing the benefits and costs of making her leave for a while. I wasn't sure my mind could become clear with her in the house, but I also wasn't sure it would become clear sitting around alone.

"Not right now, I don't. That might change at any time though."

"I understand. Whatever you need, just tell me."

I nodded my head in agreement without saying a word.

"I'll be close by," she said. "If you want to talk, just let me know."

"Thanks, Sara."

With that, she was gone again.

"Wait, where do you go when I can't see you?"

I heard only her voice, "I haven't left the house in over a year. I'm never too far away."

"So, you decide whenever you want to let me hear you or see you? I never hear you walking around; never any footsteps, no floor creaking —"

I heard her voice from the living room, somewhere behind me, "Mr. Miller."

I turned around to look but she didn't show herself. Then I heard her from the kitchen, "there are a few things you need to understand." Then, from the opposite side of the galley kitchen, "It was my body that made sounds, just like everyone else."

I stood up from the chair and walked into the main kitchen while she was talking. I heard her in the bedroom, "My body is gone." From the living room again, by the sliding door, "You may not be able to hear me," by the front door, "or see me—"

I felt a tingling sensation all over my body. Her chill was all over me. It wasn't cold, or frightening, but rather seductive. My whole body relaxed as I stood there and closed my eyes. My breathing became irregular. I felt her breath on the back of my neck, I tilted my head to the side, licked my lips and opened my mouth. I felt her cold finger on my tongue. In an instant, it all went away. I stumbled backwards when I opened my eyes and she was face to face with me, "but I'm still here." I caught myself on the counter before I fell down.

"Dammit, Sara. You scared the shit out of me. What the hell is wrong with you?"

"I don't know. I feel strange and I'm sorry, that wasn't my intention," she said as she walked towards me and leaned on the counter, facing me in her long, flowing summer dress that hugged her upper body perfectly. "If there's one thing I've learned so far, it's this. When the body can't be seen, and the voice can't be heard, the soul could still be screaming. In life, our soul communicates through our body, but in death, there are no restrictions. Yes, there are times I choose when I want you to see or hear me. Other times, my soul cries out, and there's nothing I can do to stop it."

She looked behind me, sadly, at the floor by the corner where the cabinets come together. "I just wish that was true when I was alive."

"Sara, you're going to have to learn to forgive yourself."

"How could I ever forgive myself, Toby? How?"

I stepped closer to her, put my hand on her cold chin and spoke softly, "Hey, look at me." She lifted her eyes to mine. "Only you can answer that."

I started to lean in to her and she closed her eyes softly when I realized, again, she wasn't Alex. She looked like her and talked like her, but it wasn't her. I knew quickly that, although I didn't want her to go, having Sara in the house was going to be a constant test. I was falling for Alex quickly, so I knew I had to pass that test or Sara would not just be the ghost of the house, the ghost that confessed feelings for me and that had touched me. If I allowed it—only if I allowed it, she would become the ghost of jealousy, the ghost of passion, and the ghost of my obsession; she would easily become, the ghost between us.

Chapter 18

Reunion

Keeping my mind occupied, I spent the next few days writing, fine-tuning photographs and making an occasional drive to the grocery store. I took the long way home on Thursday afternoon, so I could drive through the park. The weather was perfect. I sat at one of the stop lights in the middle of Gatlinburg and I felt my phone vibrate on my hip.

> I'm ready to talk if you are and
> if it's okay with you.   If not, I
> understand.

The light turned green before I could respond, so I waited until I stopped at the next intersection.

> Thank you, Alex.   I'm in the
> park right now on my way
> home.   Whenever you want, let
> me know when and where you
> want to meet.

> Do you have anything going on
> this afternoon?

>>> Just putting these groceries
>>> away.

> Can I come by in an hour?

>>> Absolutely.

> OK. Thank you. See you soon.

It took nearly forty minutes to get home because of the traffic in town. When I got home, I went inside and called for Sara.

I heard her distant voice, but didn't know where it came from, "Yes?"

"Alex is on her way over."

"What do you need me to do?"

"Nothing until she talks to you first, please."

"Ok."

"Ease into it, please. Don't show yourself unless it's appropriate."

"I can do that. Is she still mad?"

"I don't think so, she just sent me a message to let me know she's ready to talk."

"I knew she'd come around. That's great," she said.

I sighed before putting the last groceries in the refrigerator, "I wish I was that confident." I looked around the house to make sure it wasn't too much of a mess. There was no laundry lying around and there were vacuum cleaner marks on the carpet, so the place looked good. I made a drink for both of us (Alex and myself) and sat on the couch.

When I heard her pull up, I opened the door and she stepped into the house, cautiously looking around. I handed her the beverage I mixed for her and she immediately set it down on the counter and threw her arms around me.

"Alex, I'm really sorry, honey."

With her head still on my shoulder, she whispered, "I missed you so much."

I was beginning to relax. I had no idea what to expect so my guard was up ready for anything; anything, but that. Taking me into her arms was possibly the last scenario I would have played out in my mind if I had the time to worry about it.

"Where do you want to go?" I asked.

"Somewhere comfortable."

I led her over to the couch and we both sat down. When we did, she sat right up against me, nestled into the pocket of my shoulder with my arm around her.

I broke the silence, "Where do you want me to start?"

"Why don't you start by telling me how it began? When did you know she was here?"

She sat up on the opposite side of the couch and listened.

"It started with sounds and feelings I got, like cold chills."

"When?"

"The first night I stayed here, I got creeped out by the darkness. I've never lived in a place that gets as dark as it does around here. I got cold chills a couple of times since then. The day you came over in the rain was the first time I made contact. Anna and I did paranormal investigations a few times, so I had dowsing rods, a cryst—"

She looked at me strangely.

"Dowsing rods are skinny rods that the entity can communicate with by responding to simple, closed-ended questions." She seemed to understand, so I continued. "We have a crystal, which also only works with yes or no questions and a spirit box which allows the gho—entity to communicate verbally through the radio."

"So, you've actually spoken to her?"

"Yes, a few times. When I started with the dowsing rods—"

"Ok, enough. Just skip forward to the talking parts."

"The first time I used it, she turned it on first. It was in my closet in the room and when I heard it, I brought it out here to the table. I don't remember if she spoke first or if I did."

"But you could carry on a full conversation?"

"Not in the beginning. She wasn't strong enough. At first, she could only respond with super short answers."

"What did you talk about, Toby?"

I hesitated. I wasn't sure how she would take it, but I had kept a secret already that hurt her badly and I wasn't about to lie anymore. "You."

"What?"

"Yes, we talked about you. I asked if you knew she was here and she said you didn't and she didn't want you to know."

She became obviously angry but didn't say anything. She didn't have to. The look said it all.

"She didn't want you to know because she said it would hurt you too badly. Both of you."

She put her hand next to her face and turned away as her lip tightened.

"She watched you come and go for the last year, crying in corners and hoping you wouldn't hear her."

She took a deep breath and looked at me again, "Why is she still here?"

"She believes it's her version of Hell; her punishment for not seeing the signs of abuse when everyone else could, particularly you."

She began to cry harder, shaking her head. I didn't interrupt, but rather left her to her own thoughts. At least until I saw her shiver.

"You cold?" I asked.

"Just a chill, that's all."

She didn't notice my smile for several seconds when I didn't reply to her and she looked up at me and said, "What?" as she crossed her arms over each other, rubbing her bare arms. "Oh God, is that—is it really—"

"Yes, Alex."

She cried harder, but closed her eyes and tilted her head back, still clutching each arm for warmth.

I watched for a minute before I said, "I made her promise to ease into it, but if you want to talk—"

"Sara?" she blurted out.

"I'm right here," she said through her own cries from directly next to the couch.

Alex turned her head to the left and stood up, looking around, "Where are you? Oh, Sara, I love you. I miss you so much. I wish I could see you; touch your face and hug you one more time."

The house fell into silence. Alex began to control her emotions, still looking around, following the sound of her twin's voice. "Sara?" She looked over at me, as I stood from the couch. "Where did she go?"

"She does this a lot."

"Sara, where are you?"

Her voice came from the bedroom, "Alex, you cannot touch me. You cannot feel me other than a cold sensation. We can't hold on to each other like we used to."

I took Alex's hand and walked slowly through the living room, then in front of the bar counter. I saw a hint of a shadow stretch across the floor from behind me. I held Alex's hand tightly until we both stopped. I leaned over and whispered, "You can't touch her, Alex."

"I know."

She turned towards me, looking down with her head against my chest. I slowly turned as if slow dancing so that her back was to the bedroom and heard the elegant voice from the sliding door behind me, "Alex." With her head still in my chest, she slowly turned her head towards the door and opened her eyes with a gasp.

"Oh, Sara."

She ran over to her, but Sara put her hand out motioning her to stop just before reaching her. When she stopped, they stood facing each other for a moment, then Sara took a step forward with her hand still up and they looked deeply into each other's eyes. Alex lifted her hand to touch Sara's. She took a deep breath and pulled her other hand up to surround her sister's.

"You're so cold."

Sara smiled and lifted her hand to touch Alex's face, who shivered with chills.

Sara replied, "And you're so beautiful, as always."

"I miss you so much, Sara. I've missed you every day."

"Me too. I am so sorry I didn't let you know I was here. And I'm sorry for not letting Toby tell you."

Alex glanced over to me, "He could have told me anyway."

Sara laughed slightly, then said, "If it were me having to choose between sharing a secret like this or keeping quiet to make the woman who's haunting my house happy, I think I'd pick the latter, too."

Alex smiled, then reached out to touch Sara's face.

"We need to talk, Sissy," Alex said gently.

"What is it?"

"I just don't know how long this will last. There are things I wish I had said to you while you were—"

"It's okay, Alex. You can say it."

"When you were alive."

"Considering I have no time limit, now is as good a time as any."

They both smiled, then Alex looked over to me, "Will you excuse us please?"

"Of course, I will," I said, then walked over to kiss her, but Sara didn't move. Not wanting to feel the chill, I just touched her hand, looked at Sara and said, "Excuse me." I wondered if she was nervous about the conversation since her face showed no expression. I went into the office and sat at the computer.

I heard Alex begin, "Sara, I'm sorry I pushed you away."

"Alex, maybe I should start."

"What?"

"Daryl hit me. He beat me, he screamed at me—he was always careful not to hit me in the face where someone could see his handy work, except the nightstand incident. That was the only time he left a mark on me that couldn't be covered up. It's what we did. I egged him on just to see how far I could push him. Sometimes, I found the limit and other times—well, I crossed the line before I knew I had. He always apologized to me and told me I shouldn't push him so much, because when I did, he couldn't help himself. I knew that."

"Sara, you are not—" Alex said defiantly.

"I know I'm not responsible. I never was, but damn it felt so good to push him like that when he was pissing me off. I knew he'd scream, maybe hit me, then ignore me for several hours—which is what I wanted in the first place."

"Why didn't you leave?"

"He would have—"

There was silence for a moment, then Sara said, "Toby?"

"Yes."

"Do you mind?"

I went into the music app on my computer and started playing music but kept it low, hoping I could hear the rest of the conversation. Without touching the computer, the volume increased. I watched the volume bar at the bottom move to the right as the computer played the playlist Anna and I used to listen to in the mountains. We called it Porch Music. I couldn't hear anything else for the duration of the song. When the music faded out, I turned the volume down a little and I listened again.

"Does Toby know the truth?" Alex said.

The music came on strong with the next song. "Dammit," I said under my breath. I tried hard to hear them, but I couldn't. When that song faded out, I heard laughter, then Sara said, "I can't believe you remember that."

"How could I forget that creepy-ass jack-in-the-box?" and they laughed harder as the next song faded in. The laughter got louder as the songs transitioned from one song to the next. When there was a long pause between two songs, I turned the volume down a little more and I listened hard.

"How do I tell him, Sara?"

"Tell him what, exactly?"

The next song started before Alex responded. The pictures on the office wall began to shake. I heard a low rumble. I looked at the volume on the computer to see if it had been turned up again and the rumble was caused by the bass in the speakers, but the volume was right where I had left it. Wind blew through the house. I got up from my chair and took one step towards the door before it slammed shut in front of me. I opened it and looked into the living room. Alex was standing on her toes with her arms outstretched and her hair blowing in her face. She was screaming. The blinds closed on their own, making it darker, but there was still enough light to see.

"Alex!" I yelled. "Alex, what happened?" She quickly glanced at me as her feet flattened on the floor. My vision was blurry and I rubbed my eyes to clear them. I looked again with wide eyes. There seemed to be two versions of Alex; one superimposed on top of the other thrashing about; neither of them in sync with the other.

"Alex!" I yelled one more time before the shock of the reality hit me with clear realization. I stepped forward slowly and said calmly, "Sara?" They both fixed their eyes on me from the same body; Alex's body. "Sara, what have you done?"

"What does it matter to you?" she said angrily. "You should be asking, what has *she* done?"

I reached my hand out to her, "Okay, Sara, what has she done?" Alex's body was still moving around unnaturally when I reached them. "What did Alex do, Sara? Let's talk."

She reached her hand out to mine and our fingers joined. The wind stopped, the rumbling settled. Everything in the house stopped shaking. Alex's face calmed into a sympathetic expression, but it was Sara's voice I heard, "Oh my God, Toby, I can feel you."

My heart raced, and I felt my blood pressure rise as I let go.

"Get out."

Her eyes were sad, and she reached for me again.

"I said, GET OUT, SARA!"

She vanished, and Alex collapsed to the floor with a thud. In an instant, I knelt down by her side, touching her arms, her face, and her neck. I brushed the hair from her face and called out her name.

"Alex. Alex, sweetheart. I'm right here. It's okay, baby. I'm right here."

Her eyes squinted a few times without opening. Her face expressed discomfort. She breathed hard a few times, licked her lips and opened her eyes slowly. "Where is she?"

"She's gone."

"Why?"

"Uh, tell me what happened."

"We were laughing, and I needed to ask her something."

She sat up, leaning on her outstretched hand, but looked around, trying to recall the events.

"I asked her—and she—she got mad and—"

She looked at me intensely.

"Are you fucking kidding me right now?"

"What?" I asked.

Alex continued, "She leaned over to me and before I knew it, I was standing up, but I didn't have to move a muscle, it just happened. That fucking bitch. She fucking possessed me. I mean, are you serious right now? What the f—"

"She's gone now, Alex."

"What made her leave?"

"I did. I told her to get out."

She stood up and started yelling again, "SARA! SARA! WHERE ARE YOU? DON'T THINK I WON'T EXERCISE YOUR DEMON ASS, YOU LITTLE BITCH!"

She looked over at me, "I cannot believe she did that to me."

I walked over to her and put my hand gently on her back. She calmed slightly and took deep breaths.

"What made her so mad, Alex? What did you ask her?"

She looked around, but not at me.

"Alex, what did you ask?"

She exhaled heavily, put her hand on my chest and said, "I asked her how I should tell you."

"Tell me what?"

She was still trying to catch her breath when she finally said, "That I'm falling in love with you."

Chapter 19

Haunted

"Wow Alex," I smiled. "I have to give it to you straight here."

"Oh no, Toby. I'm sorry. Don't say anything, please. Just don't say it."

"I have to say just this. The words are far easier to transition than the emotion is right now. I mean, your sister just—you know. Shit was blowing all over the house and damn near shaking off the walls."

She smiled back at me briefly, and said, "I know. I'm just telling you what happened and why she got so mad." She was still out of breath from running around the house, chasing after Sara. We both walked around to different areas of the house looking for signs of her. We ended our search in the spare room.

"Anything?" I asked.

"Nothing, you?"

"No—just that," I said, pointing to the jack-in-the-box on the nightstand.

Alex walked around the bed, grabbed the toy by the clown's head and walked out the sliding door from the living room. When she was clear into the grass, she pulled it next to her head and launched it into the edge of the woods. She walked back in, slid the door closed and sat on the couch. I walked over to sit next to her. Both of us were still cautiously looking around the house but leaned back trying to relax.

"Well?" she said.

"Well what?"

"No other comments?"

I turned slightly towards her and took her hands in mine. "Alex, I've kept secrets from you and I'm sorry for that. I will not do it again. To express my feelings is one thing; to say it out loud is something different, you know?"

I pulled her hands up to my face and kissed them. "I hope you feel it, baby. I really do. Please tell me you feel it."

"Toby, I've never felt so much love from a man in all my life. I've had plenty of people say it, but I've never felt it like I do with you. You don't have to say it. Not yet."

She smiled and continued, "But a girl does like to hear it out loud sometimes."

"I know," I said as I leaned back, still holding one of her hands.

"I can't believe she did that."

"Did she have anger issues when she was alive?" I asked.

"She did a little when we were kids, but she learned to suppress it."

"I'd say, years of suppression were just released in my damn living room."

She shook her head several times and I didn't need to ask why.

"Tob—" she started, then took a few deep breaths. She finally looked over at me and said, "I'm not sure I can stay here."

"It's okay. I'm not so sure I can either."

"Where is she? Where does she go?"

"She said she can't leave the house. She's never been outside since. She said that when you come over, she stays in the basement sometimes."

"Did you check there?"

"Yes, I did. I think you were looking in the bedroom when I went downstairs."

We both looked at the floor and occasionally around the room. Alex sighed and said, "I have to go, Toby. I'm sorry, but I really don't feel safe here."

"I get it but keep your phone nearby in case I call in the middle of the night." I smiled at my own fear.

"You've got yourself a deal."

"Besides, I want to be here when she comes back."

"You really think she'll come back?"

I thought about the last thing Sara said. She could feel me. It calmed her.

"Yes," I said quietly as I looked around the house. "I'm certain of it."

I walked her out the front door and to her car. I held her close to me, kissed her then opened her door for her. Her window was down. She started the car and asked, "Let me know when she shows up again?"

"Oh, you'll be the first call I make. It might be a while. She's weak. She disappears every time she gets emotional. She compares it to being completely exhausted while she was alive. The first night I talked to her with the spirit box when she only responded with short phrases, her voice was fading after only a short time. I'm telling you, it will be at least a day before I hear anything from her."

"Just call me when you do please."

"I will. Be careful driving home. It looks like it could storm."

"Okay. Bye, Toby."

I smiled and watched her pull away before going back into the house. I locked the door behind me and stepped into the living room, then walked around to straighten every picture and pick up the little things that blew over in the chaos. With the combination of clouds rolling in and dusk approaching, I turned on some lights and made a sandwich. Every sound in the house made me flinch, from the distant thunder to slight creaking sounds from the floor. The wind began to blow against the back of the house. I walked to the sliding door and a flash of lightning lit up the ominous black sky, making the edges of the thick clouds visible briefly. It hadn't even started raining yet.

> You make it home yet?

> Just pulled in the garage and
> turned off the car.

> OK. Glad you made it.

> Thanks for checking on me.

The wind picked up and the lights flickered. I lit several candles around the house just in time before the power went out. I looked around the house again, suspiciously, and closed all of the blinds just as the thunder rolled through the valley and echoed off the mountains. I pulled up the weather app on my phone. The storm was supposed to last for several hours but become clear before morning.

I went through the sliding door in the bedroom under the enclosed patio to watch the storm roll in. The wind speed continued to increase, and the lightning flashed more frequently. I heard the unmistakable distant sound of pouring rain moving quickly towards me through the woods. When it reached the tree line and continued towards me, the trees began to fade then just before it blanketed the patio, the trees had completely disappeared.

I went inside and looked around the house for leaks with a large flashlight. The rain that fell the week before wasn't nearly as hard as this time. I looked at the roof all around the edges of the ceiling on the outer walls. When I found none, I went to the basement. There was standing water already on the concrete patio just outside the sliding door, but it wasn't coming in. I checked closely around the theater room and the area where my drum set was sitting; all of it was dry. I opened the door to the garage and shined the flashlight around the overhead door which was also dry. I walked back upstairs, comforted that the house was well-sealed, blew out all but one candle and carried the last one to my bedroom.

The flashes were constant; as was the rolling thunder, interrupted only by brighter flashes and cracks of thunder that would make an artilleryman flinch. I laid on my bed just to relax and listen to the storm roll through. Even through closed eyes, I could see the flashes of lightning. After a few minutes, the rain lightened, the darkness between flashes became longer and the thunder tamed to a constant growl through the valley. The more I laid there, the more relaxed I became until I felt something. I wasn't startled, just maybe a little surprised.

Her fingertips drew circles on my chest. I could feel her against me with her bare leg bent and her knee across my legs.

"What are you doing?" I whispered.

"Shh, what does it feel like I'm doing?"

Even with her leg across me, I felt weightless. Her imaginary circles became larger, reaching up the side of my neck. I stretched it to the side with a quiet moan. I felt kisses; kisses on my hand, my arm, my shoulder, my ear, my chest, then my stomach. I drew a breath and reached down to run my fingers through her hair. She eased her body up to match mine. I felt something drip on the side of my face and reached up with my right hand to wipe it off. Before I could focus on it, I felt another drip and another, wiping them off after every one of them. I looked at my fingers by the dim light of the candle. It was red and warm.

"Blood? What the fuck!"

It dripped faster on to me. I tried to move but couldn't. I felt trapped on my own bed. When I could finally turn my head upwards, I saw Sara hovering above me with blood dripping out of the corner of her mouth and oozing out of her left shoulder. I screamed, and she was gone.

I looked at my hand, which was as clean as it was when I laid down. I felt my face. There were no drips anywhere. I sat up in the bed. The lights around the house had come back on. I jumped out of bed and looked at the sheets. They were clean. I walked out the sliding door from the bedroom and looked around at a clear, starry sky. It wasn't until then that I looked at the clock. It was 3:30 in the morning so I paced the house with a glass of water and the lights on, trying to shake off the nightmare.

I heard the floor creak in the kitchen.

"Sara, is that you?" I said cautiously. I was no longer convinced that Sara was the sweet, elegant person I was led to believe she was. "Sara, where are you?"

I went into the bedroom closet and pulled all of the equipment out of the box to take it to the dining room.

"Do you remember these?" I said when I held up the dowsing rods. "Let's see if we can talk a little. I know you're not strong. I'm sure it took a lot of energy to do what you did earlier. I held the rods straight in front of me, mid-torso. "Are you here?"

"Sara, are you okay?"

I walked around to different areas of the house, but never got another response.

"I know, let's try the crystal. Maybe that will be easier for you to move."

I took the crystal out of the box and held it straight out in front of me by the long, gold chain attached to it, and waited for it to stop moving.

"Sara, can you move the crystal? Even if you just tap it, it will move."

There was no response. I started yawning so I tried to lay down again to try and get a few more hours of sleep. Just before I did, I looked at my phone. There was a text message from Alex that she sent around 1:30.

I can't sleep.

I hesitated, but sent a reply anyway

You still awake?

Broken sleep. I am right now.

I just had an awful nightmare.
It was terrible.

What was it?

Not even sure I'm ready to
share yet. I'll tell you next time
I see you.

Any signs?

Nothing. I'm going to try to get
back to sleep myself.
Goodnight.

I blew out the candle on the nightstand and rolled over with all the lights still on.

The next time I woke up, it was almost 10:00. I laid there thinking of the nightmare and about what happened in my own living room the day before. I looked at my fingertips and rubbed them together, still feeling the silky-smooth sensation of the dripping blood from my dream. I looked over at my phone but there were no new notifications, so I got up to shower. I was still creeped out, so I wiped the steam off the glass shower door several times. After the third time clearing a spot where I could see through the glass, I wondered if I was doing it because I hoped I wouldn't see her or because I wanted to.

I became more comfortable throughout the day after drinking coffee and sitting outside a few times. I sent Alex a message soon after my shower asking her to let me know when she's up. It was 2:30 before I got a response that she was but was going to clean up before calling me.

Trying to keep my mind occupied was futile. I wasn't comfortable listening to music because I wouldn't be able to hear Sara when she returned. I thought about woodworking in the detached garage but knew I would get the same results. I considered watching a movie, playing the drums; everything I considered took away from the silence I wanted and needed so badly. I can't explain why I suddenly felt so uncomfortable. Sure, I watched a possession in my living room the day before and I had a ghastly nightmare that kept me up for a while, but the discomfort I felt wasn't reminiscent of past events. It was—something; something I can't explain to this day, but it was certainly real.

I paced the house most of the day trying to pinpoint the origin of my feelings, but nothing made sense. It was like the feeling that someone was watching me or that there was a ghost in the house. Been there. I could definitely mark that off of my list of things to do. I lived with a ghost watching me for weeks and never felt like I did that day. Discomfort turned to fear, and fear into terror when I walked outside from the basement, leaving the sliding door open only a few inches.

It started out pleasant enough. The sun was shining, the breeze was light, and the air was a perfect temperature. I only stood there for a few moments before I sensed something from behind me. When I turned around, chills covered my body. I was petrified with my body frozen but my mind as sharp as ever. I saw nothing but my own reflection in the clear glass. A blackness filled the basement. I couldn't see anything inside. The sliding door was still opened a few inches, but I didn't dare reach for the handle. I stood, expressionless, until the hold was released from the sinister invitation.

Chapter 20

Blackened

You're back in your cold, dark theater
This time it's for real.
You try to put it on paper
But can't explain how you feel.

A nothing, yet a something
A cold, but yet a warmth.
You stare into the nothing
Afraid to go forth.

All of time has frozen
But you have to play your part.
A nothing has taken your sight
And a something has taken your heart.

This is the place where the two worlds meet
A sliding door between the two.

You try to take control of the moment
But it seems the moment has control of you.

As the nothing returns your stare
You know that you've been beat.
For a moment you are taken prisoner
By the something where the two worlds meet.

I conjured every bit of courage I had, took a deep breath, slid the door open and stepped into the theater room. Although still tense, the air was clear. When I closed the door behind me, the house was as silent as death itself. I looked around with only my eyes and slowly stepped further into the basement. I nearly jumped out of my skin when my phone vibrated on my hip.

"Hello."

"Anything?" Alex asked.

"That's a bit relative now."

"What do you mean?"

"Something just doesn't feel right."

"Is she there?"

"I'm not sure. I've never felt this way in this place before."

"I'm coming over."

She ended the call and I walked around the house with all of my senses piqued. I wandered around the basement looking for anything that looked out of place. I opened the garage door slowly, scanned it for the same, but didn't see anything unusual. I walked upstairs and stopped at the top of the steps. I heard frequent noises in different parts of the house but couldn't make out what they were.

"Sara?" I began to call out in each room. "Where are you?"

I kept going to the front door to see when Alex would arrive, but I knew it would be at least another ten minutes. I checked the bathroom, the closets and anywhere else that wasn't immediately visible.

What was that darkness? Why is it happening now? Is it Sara at all? I've never felt that way before; a whole new level of fright.

I stepped outside again to try to recreate the situation upstairs. Although I didn't want to see that again, I had to know if it was truly gone. Clouds were rolling in, eliminating shadows, but it wasn't a storm. I looked around the backyard and nothing appeared to be strange or unusual. The hot tub cycled as always, and the air conditioner came on, but other than that, there were no sounds before I heard a noise coming from the woods, like sticks snapping.

I walked closer to the tree line slowly. If it was the bear with her cubs, I certainly didn't want to startle her. I got all the way into the wide path towards the gazebo. I heard the sound a few more times. It wasn't some distant noise. It was somewhere close to me; within fifty feet, for sure, but there was nothing there. I didn't see any squirrels, chipmunks, bears or any other critter, for that matter.

I heard a gunshot coming from the house and sprinted to see what was going on. I ran into the house and straight to the front door. Alex wasn't even there yet. My heart was racing faster than ever before. I felt as though the sound of my heartbeat was echoing through the house. I heard a creaking sound to my right and looked over to see the open corner cabinet door.

I opened the front door as soon as I heard Alex's tires rolling on the gravel. When I did, there was peace. All of the noises stopped and there was no tension in the air anymore. I closed the corner cabinet and leaned on the counter, taking deep breaths trying to regulate my heartbeat. It slowed gradually until I no longer felt it was echoing through the house. I heard two birds chirping from somewhere in the front yard when Alex turned her car off and got out.

"Anything yet?" she asked through the screen door.

"I haven't seen her."

"What were you talking about that you felt earlier?"

I didn't answer her. She reached the steps to come in. I instantly got a different feeling, as if I were some type of bait for a trap. Everything went silent again and seemed to move in slow motion. She reached the top of the steps and I looked around the house again curiously. Anxiety washed over me when she reached for the handle of the screen door to pull it towards her. She stepped through the door and walked towards me. When she got two steps into the house, all hell broke loose.

The front door slammed shut behind her, the cabinet doors opened and closed repeatedly. There was a roaring sound throughout the house, like the one I heard before. Framed pictures rattled on the walls. The blinds closed. The house fell into total darkness, just like the basement, which made my first night in the house seem as though I slept in the middle of the afternoon. Alex screamed and reached for me. Her fingertips swiped my arm several times, so I reached for her and she started to cry. Wind blew through the house. Alex yelled so that I could hear her, "Why is she doing this? Why?"

I could tell we were facing each other when both of our hands grasped the other's arms.

"Get down on the floor," I yelled. "Get behind the counter."

She crawled towards the kitchen on her hands and knees and I was right behind her with my hand on her ankle so I wouldn't lose her.

"Ouch, ouch, ahh," she said as the doors repeatedly swung open, hitting her.

"Try to lean against the doors."

We both sat upright and leaned our backs against the cabinet doors, which held shut with our weight against them.

"I can't see a damn thing," I yelled.

Alex screamed, "Why are you doing this? Stop, please."

The house fell silent—except for our breathing, but the darkness remained. I leaned over to look around the counter.

"Where are you going? Don't leave me," Alex begged.

I whispered, "I'm just trying to see if there's light coming from anywhere. I'm not going anywhere."

I leaned out again.

"What do you see?"

"Nothing at all."

I heard a tapping sound on the tile floor in the galley kitchen.

"What was that?" she asked in a panic.

"I don't know. We need to get outside or at least open the door."

"Don't leave me."

"Honey, I'm going right over to the front door. I won't be far. When I open the door, the darkness will go away."

"How do you know?"

"I saw it in the basement a few hours ago. Now, stay right here."

"Okay. I will."

I slowly leaned to my left side and pulled my feet up underneath me. Alex was touching me the whole time. I felt around for the cabinets on the opposite side of the kitchen and followed them to the end, then reached for the front door. I couldn't quite reach the door with my foot stretched back as far as I could so that Alex knew exactly where I was. I leaned back and whispered, "You're going to have to move with me or let go. I'm inches away from reaching the door, but I can't quite get it unless you move."

"I can't, Toby. I can't move."

"Because something has you or because you're too scared?"

"I'm scared. I'm so scared. Just reach out, open the door quickly and come right back."

"Look, if I can get the door open I won't need to crawl back because it will be gone."

"Okay, hurry, Toby."

"I will."

I crawled across the tile floor again with my hand brushing the cabinets leading to the front door. Alex touched my ankle for as long as possible. When I had to reach, I turned around to her and said, "Ready?"

"Hurry."

I pulled my foot from her grip and in one motion, reached for the front door, but it was locked. I reached up quickly to unlock the deadbolt, grabbed the door knob and pulled as hard as I could. When I did, my body flew through the air backwards.

"TOBY!" Alex screamed when I yelled from being launched across the room.

"Where are you?" she cried.

"Best I can tell, I think I'm across the living room."

I took a few deep breaths and quickly crawled towards where I believed the sliding door was. It was at an angle, but I found the glass, felt around until I found the long handle. I felt behind the handle to make sure it was unlocked and pulled. It didn't move.

Alex screamed, "GET OFF ME! WHAT ARE YOU DOING?"

I sat on the floor against the glass and yelled out, "ALEX!"

She was crying and sounded like she was choking at the same time.

"Alex, what's going on?" I shouted. "LET HER GO."

She gasped for air and swallowed hard several times before she said in a scratchy voice, "She just choked me," and moaned loudly each time she exhaled.

I used my elbow and started pounding on the glass, but it was too thick and I couldn't break it. Out of breath, I sat down, leaning against the glass again. "Alex, just stay right there."

I took deep breaths as my mind raced, trying to think of heavy objects that might be near me. I felt around the carpet, patting every few inches, and realized how quiet it had become.

"Alex? Alex. ALEX!"

The sound came from the bedroom as far as I could tell; the distinct first few notes sounded from the jack-in-the-box. I heard Alex cry out again, but it sounded like she was in the basement.

"ALEX!"

I crawled around on the ground, trying to reach the bedroom. I felt the floor change from the carpet to tile at the edge of the dining room. Every few feet, I stopped and waved my hand in front of me to ensure the path was still clear.

"WHAT DO YOU WANT? WHY ARE YOU DOING THIS?" I shouted as loudly as I could. Just as I was about to reach the bedroom, I felt my ankle being grabbed and I was dragged backwards across the floor until my feet hit the wall by the spare bedroom. My chest burned from my shirt lifting up and the friction of my chest against the carpet.

"Where is she?" I pleaded. "What did you do with her? ANSWER ME, DAMMIT!"

A few more notes played from the jack-in-the-box, now right next to me, it seemed. I felt around the wall. I was between the spare bedroom and the bathroom.

"SERAPHINA, GET OUT OF MY HOUSE!" I yelled.

The light blinded me. I squinted my eyes, blinking fast to adjust to the sunlight that filled the room again.

I yelled for Alex, "Where are you?" I heard her crying from a distance.

"I'm in the basement."

"Can you see?"

"Yes, sort of. My eyes are still adjusting."

I stumbled to my feet and looked around the house again. Some of my prints had shaken completely off the walls; the rest were hanging unevenly. I held my arm over my eyes, still adjusting to the light. Three more terrifying notes played.

"SARA! SARA!"

As my eyes began to adjust, I looked around the living room, then down the narrow galley kitchen. I got to the top of the stairs and yelled, "Are you okay, Alex?"

"Yes, just come down here."

"I'll be right there."

I went into my bedroom and looked around but saw nothing. Things were shaken up there too. I went back to the spare room where I heard the toy the loudest. On the opposite side of the bed, she was there, crouched upon the floor as weak as I've ever seen.

"Sara, you have to stop this."

She looked up at me terrified and whispered, "Get Alex out of here."

"Why? What's going on?"

"It's not me, Toby."

I looked at her, puzzled for a moment until she expounded, "It's my husband."

Chapter 21
Uninvited

For the first time since I had been there, my forever house became my living nightmare. I'd been startled over the past weeks by my own imagination's reaction to events in the house; conjuring images of monsters that didn't exist. When Sara told me that, I was numb. My imagination no longer played a part. I couldn't just shake it off and convince myself that it was all in my head, and there was no reasoning with the creator of the mayhem that had riddled my house in the last twenty-four hours. It was pure rage from an unseen entity; an entity powerful enough to blacken the brightest day, create a windstorm from nothing, kidnap my girlfriend and throw me across the room.

I stared at Sara's feeble apparition, trying to dismiss the frightened feeling that washed over me. "Where is he?" I whispered.

Fright turned into terror when she said shakily, "He's everywhere."

I ran out of the room and down the steps to the basement. "Alex, come on."

"Where are we going?"

"I need to get you out of here."

"I'm not leaving you. What the hell's going on?"

"It's not Sara, Alex."

"What? Then who is it?"

"It's Daryl."

I reached out to grab her, but she ran past me so fast, I couldn't stop her from running up the stairs.

She yelled through her cries, "Where are you, you son of a bitch?"

She screamed, and I heard a loud thud before I reached the door at the top of the steps. She was on the living room floor, curled up in a protective, fetal position with her mouth forced shut. Painful tears fell out of the sides of her eyes.

"Let her go, Daryl," I said firmly, but somewhat calmly.

Alex opened her mouth in relief and rolled onto her back.

As quickly as the smoky figure appeared, he sped towards me and stopped, an inch from my face. He was a dirty looking man with a stubbly beard and disheveled hair. His eyes were crazed, and he tilted his head from side to side, inspecting me.

"And, who do we have here?" he said.

I didn't say anything at first; just returned his black-eyed stare.

"Oh, wait. We've met a couple of times today, haven't we? I'm—"

"I know who you are, you murdering fucking bastard."

He danced around the living room laughing and shouting, "We have a winner, ladies and gentlemen," just before the distorted notes played again from the jack-in-the-box and he sang along, "Pop goes the weasel."

Alex's body lifted off the ground with the first note and slammed hard against the ceiling.

"LEAVE HER ALONE," I yelled.

He stopped, looked over at me and calmly said, "Okay," and her body dropped eight feet onto the floor. I ran over to her and took her hand.

"Oh, really now? What do we have here? Our own Mister Miller has fallen for my whore sister-in-law. So, tell me, Tobias, how is it that you have such anger for me and call me—wait, how did you put it? Oh yeah, a murdering fucking bastard, but you have fallen for another, just like me, you hypocritical fuck."

I looked at Alex and she shook her head back and forth slowly.

"WHOA!" he said. "Do you mean to tell me that our lovely Toby doesn't know? In the dark? Again?" He laughed at himself and said, "You must like the dark, my friend." He bent down and whispered in Alex's ear, "Why don't you tell our friend here what you did?"

I heard a frail voice from the spare bedroom, "No."

He jumped up and tilted his head back and forth, darting his eyes from side to side; his expression blank. "Sara?" He looked at me with a smile, "Speaking of whores."

Alex looked up at him from the floor, "Don't you call her that," but he was gone.

"Alex," Sara called.

"Sissy, where are you?"

"I'm in here."

She stood up and walked into the spare bedroom. "Sara," she gasped. "What can I do?"

"I need you."

"Anything. Anything at all. What do you need?"

"I need your strength."

"Sara, you are strong. You've always been. You just need to believe
—" She stopped talking when Sara shook her head.

"I need the strength of your body."

"You mean, like yesterday?"

"Yes."

"I don't know, Sara. I just—how can you even consider that. It's
what caused you to be so weak in the first place."

"I know, but we can do this together. We can do anything together."

"You know how to get rid of him?"

"Yes."

I stood in the doorway in disbelief of what I was hearing. "Alex, I
don't know if—"

"I have to, Toby. It may be our only chance."

Sara smiled slightly as she stood up.

"What do I need to do?" Alex asked.

"Just lay down on the bed and close your eyes."

Alex cautiously walked next to the bed, sat on the edge and looked at
Sara.

"Are you sure about this?" I asked.

Alex looked at me with determination. "Yes," she replied. "I'm
certain of it," then laid back on the bed and closed her eyes.

I watched, amazed as Sara stood strongly, turned her back to the bed
and sat down in the middle of her sister's body. Alex took a deep breath.
Sara slowly pulled her feet up on the bed, one at a time, lining them up
with Alex's. Sara folded her arms in front of her and began to lay back.
Her waist disappeared into Alex's; then her stomach followed by her
shoulders.

"What can I do?" I asked.

Sara looked at me with an angry look. Her eyes turned black just before she disappeared completely into her sister and Alex's body raised up with insanity in her blackened eyes when I heard Daryl's voice, "Get out of my goddamn house."

He jumped at me as I watched Sara's face protruding from Alex, trying to break herself free. He tackled me to the floor near the fireplace with his sinister eyes inches from mine looking from Alex's beautiful face and his hands around my throat. He lifted my head by my neck and slammed it against the floor. I grabbed the fire iron from beside me and said, "I'm so sorry, Alex" before hitting him on the head with it. He rolled off me and I stood up. I crouched slightly wielding the iron like a shotgun and said, "Come on, Motherfucker."

He stood up straight and laughed at me. I pulled the iron back as far as I could to get the most possible force, knowing he was going to try to block it. I swung it as fast as a baseball bat with all my strength. But he didn't block it. He held his hands up and laughed harder. I tried to stop the swing, but it was too late; it landed hard on Alex's ribs, completely unblocked. As Alex's screamed, I simultaneously heard Sara crying and Daryl shouting, "HOLY COW, IT'S A HOME RUN!"

He came at me again and tried to swing his fist at me. Alex's eyes returned briefly and she held her fist back and yelled, "NO."

Her face went stone cold again and eyes faded to black. She put her arms up and out to her sides and things flew at me from everywhere in the room. I pulled my arms up in front of my face for protection. Objects hit me from all sides. I felt myself getting dizzy and dropped to the ground in front of the spare room, still protecting myself as much as I could. My eyes were burning from the pain in my head and I raised my hand slightly in surrender.

Everything stopped. I slowly lowered my arms from my face, out of breath. When the house was calm again, I took deep breaths.

"Toby, my man, you don't know what you're doing," he continued through Alex. Sara's face stopped trying to escape. "Let me fill you in."

"Daryl, I don't really give a shit what happened."

"Oh, that's too bad. I was really excited to bring you into our little circle."

I was beaten and exhausted, so I didn't reply.

He started his story, "I had just come home from work expecting a nice home-cooked meal, since that's her job and shit, you know?"

He paced in the living room. "To my, not so big fucking surprise, she hadn't done shit." He ran over, leaned into my face and screamed, "nothing, Toby." I looked into eyes that flickered from Alex to Sara, then back to his own; blacked out and evil. His voice calmed, "Not a fucking thing," then laughed angrily.

He stood up again walked to the middle of the living room with his hands out and yelled, "I mean, come on! Where's the respect for the man? She promised to honor and obey—but there was none of that shit."

I laid there not saying a thing and he continued.

"She stood in the kitchen."

He walked through the dining room and looked into the kitchen recalling the events.

"Miss Proper," he said sarcastically, "grew a set of balls the size of The Titanic. She started crying and said she loved her sister and that she missed her."

Without touching it, he launched a chair at me.

"I asked her what the hell her sister had to do with this. She told me that she felt like a prisoner in her own home and that wasn't fair."

His mocking cry turned into a laugh. "It wasn't fair. Let's talk about fair for a minute, Mister Miller."

He walked over to me, put the chair upright and sat in it. "I'm guessing you're a respectable guy who understands what's REQUIRED —of a woman." He smiled down at me and turned his head side to side again. "Hmm, Toby? You understand, right? I'm sure your lovely Anna obeyed your every wish, didn't she?"

"You leave Anna out of this, asshole."

He lifted a single finger and waved it back and forth. "Wrong answer, Toby. Wrong answer."

With that, I flew into the nightstand next to the bed in the spare bedroom. I couldn't see him anymore, but he continued, "SHE TOLD ME—that she wasn't going to take my shit any longer and that I needed to leave."

I heard glass shattering, "CAN YOU BELIEVE IT, MAN? SHE ASKED ME TO LEAVE. I had to remind her who was in charge—so I taught her a little respect." He laughed. "Several times."

I leaned on the nightstand, thinking hard about how I could get him out of my house. I thought of The Cashtown Inn when we watched a medium help a soldier cross over. The soldier was reasonable and listened to the medium. I knew I didn't have a chance in hell of anything like that working. I thought of the television shows where they read from the Bible to expel the entities. With no Bible nearby, I knew that wasn't an option either. Then it came to me as if it were obvious. I noticed the fire iron laying on the floor near the fireplace. There was only one way I was going to be able to stop him—but I needed that fire iron.

"YOU STILL WITH ME, TOBY?" I heard him yell. He was pacing back and forth between the kitchen and the dining room and continued, "I walked away from her. I figured that she had learned her lesson, so I turned away to go to the basement. All was fine until Alex got involved."

He was getting angrier by the minute.

"She stepped into the kitchen with her sister and thought it would be a good idea to tell me she was taking Sara away and there was nothing I could do about it." He paused, then said, "I had no idea the bitch was even here."

I shouted at him, "Don't call her that, you dick."

The fire iron straightened so it was pointing directly at me and flew through the air. I leaned towards the bed as it hit the nightstand exactly where my head was, then it dropped to the floor next to me.

"Shut it, Toby," he said from the other room. "I'm not done."

I looked down at the fire iron as he continued, "I never looked back until I heard the hammer clicks behind me." He yelled again, "I pulled my pistol from my hip, turned around to take my shot and got the surprise of my life."

I crouched down so that I was lying flat on the floor and looked under the bed.

He spoke softly, "Sara was pointing a pistol at me when my bullet hit her in the chest."

I slowly reached for the fire iron and shifted it, inch by inch until it was under the bed.

He sounded sad when he said, "She stumbled backwards and fell back into the corner where the cabinets come together, right here. I screamed at Alex when she dropped down to help her sister. THAT BITCH IS THE REASON MY WIFE IS DEAD, TOBY."

I watched carefully but didn't see him. I only heard him sniffling. I grabbed the fire iron and reached it across under the bed, hooked it around the jack-in-the-box and pulled it towards me.

"I dropped my gun on the floor, right here and slid down the stone wall," I heard him say. "I sat here—crying—with my head between my knees and heard a sucking sound as my wife took her last breaths."

I sat up, positioning the toy directly in front of me with the clown popped out, smiling at me.

"I pulled my head from my knees to take one last look at my wife and, for a fraction of a second, I actually saw the bullet coming straight for me after Alex fired the shot."

He stood in the doorway to the spare bedroom as I lifted the iron above my head.

"SHE FUCKING MURDERED ME, TOBY—what are you doing?"

I hit the clown directly with all my strength. Sara started to break free. I watched their torsos separate as Alex fell to the ground, Daryl screamed in pain and Sara cried out. I pulled the iron over my head and dropped it down again. Sara laid on the floor briefly before disappearing. Daryl crawled out of Alex's body towards the toy but vanished before he reached it. Alex looked up at me, sobbing. I put the iron down and held her close to me.

"It's over, baby, it's over."

I rocked her back and forth and held her tightly until her hysterics calmed to a gentle cry.

Chapter 22

Roommate

"Where's Sara?" she asked.

"She'll be back. It might take a while though. Think of what she's been through."

"I don't want to."

The sun was setting when we stood up and walked to the sliding door in the living room. She winced with every step, holding her left side. We stopped so I could look at her side. The bruise was huge and was already dark. She leaned into me with her head on my shoulder as we looked at the orange glow in the sky. I slid the door open and we stepped out onto the patio. Birds were chirping. Three deer looked up at us from behind the detached garage. Mama bear walked across the back of the property and into the four-wheeler path with her three cubs close behind.

"It doesn't seem right," she said.

"What's that, baby?"

"It's so peaceful out here after what we've just been through."

I turned my head and looked through the glass door. The pictures that hadn't fallen were crooked on the wall. Objects were scattered across the floor; some broken. I noticed a frame upside down in the middle of the floor and turned.

"Where are you going?" Alex asked.

"Just right in here. I'll be right back."

"You've said that before. I don't like it."

I turned to face her, "It's over, honey. It's really over. It's okay." I rubbed my hand gently down her arm and took her hand and we walked into the living room together. I reached down to pick up the frame and turned it over. It was the first picture Anna and I took in the park a few days after our wedding, sitting on a large rock with the water cascading around us. I placed it on one of the cabinets neatly. Alex walked over to one of the pictures and straightened it on the wall, then stepped in front of another and did the same. I picked up one of the large prints off the floor and hung it back in its place. Alex took my arm when I straightened it, smiled at me and said, "Reagan's Mill."

We continued picking things up off the floor and straightening things that hadn't fallen. Little by little, the house started to look normal again. We turned some lights on and continued until the whole house was clean. When it was, we took a flashlight out to the fire pit outside and started a small fire with paper towels and small sticks. We gathered kindling and put it on the fire until it was burning on its own and put a few larger sticks and small logs on it. When it was high enough, we walked inside the house and got the small bag off the counter to take it back to the fire.

"Burn in hell, you son of a bitch," she said when I dumped the shattered jack-in-the-box into the fire and put a few more logs onto the fire to keep it going. We walked back into the house, turned on the rest of the lights and went to bed.

When we woke the next morning, we brewed coffee and walked out to the fire. There was nothing left but ashes, so we went back to sit in the rocking chairs on the enclosed patio next to the hot tub.

"I'm sorry, Toby."

"For what?"

"For lying to you about that night."

I reached for her hand, "Look, I'd be perfectly fine if we never spoke of that night again."

"But, I think I need to."

I looked at her and she smiled at me before she continued, "I just need to know we're okay. I thought that if you knew what I had done—"

"Alex, you protected your sister."

"No, Toby, I didn't. She was already gone when I shot him. I killed him, Toby."

"How did you win your case? Temporary insanity?"

"There was no case. You're not in Indiana anymore. Daryl was an asshole and everyone knew it. He kept to himself and wasn't friends with anybody."

"But he had a job."

"I know. A couple of weeks after, I called the place he worked. They told me he quit. Just never showed up one day and they hadn't seen him since."

"What about the obituary? There was no mention of him at all."

"No, there wasn't, was there. At the time, Sara Reagan didn't exist. I didn't report it with her married name."

"So, no one knew what happened?"

"Everyone knew what happened, Toby."

224

"I don't understand."

"Everyone knows everyone around here and domestic violence isn't reported. We tend to take matters into our own hands, so to speak. The police, the funeral home, the coroner—they all know the truth. We had her funeral on a remote property. It was never published until the day after so that no one would come."

"No one was at her funeral?"

She took a sip of her coffee and looked up at the ceiling with a sigh.

"What?" I asked.

"Ninety-eight people attended her funeral that day. It lasted for six hours so that the visitors were spread out and the traffic wouldn't bring attention to the service. Every time someone said they were sorry for my loss, they followed it with a 'Thank you,' especially the police. He was a bad man, Toby. This town just let him—disappear."

"Wow," I whispered as I sipped my coffee. "How do you deal with that?"

"It took a while. I watched my back for a long time before I was finally comfortable with it. I haven't lost a minute of sleep since then. I'm at peace with it. Well, I was until yesterday afternoon, but I'm okay again."

She pulled my hand up to kiss it.

"Hey," she said.

I turned to her.

"I love you, Tobias Miller. Thank you for keeping me at peace. I will forever be in your debt."

I smiled at her and said, "Uh, yes. Yes, you will."

We sat quietly for a while until she asked me, "How did you know it was the jack-in-the-box?"

"There's always a portal of some kind."

She looked confused.

"Think about it. Sara never left. Daryl did. When an entity is brought into a house, it's either invited or released somehow. That's why you'll never see me anywhere near a Ouija board. People don't get to choose who they communicate with. They just open a portal that can let anything through. It wasn't a coincidence that Daryl was here. He wasn't invited, so he had to come through some type of portal. Ever since Sara opened the jack-in-the-box, shit's gotten weird around here. I heard more noises, not to mention that awful nightmare. I just felt uneasy."

"You can feel a presence?" she asked.

"To some extent, yes. I even saw a full apparition on the Battlefield at Gettysburg once—I think of him a lot."

"In what way?"

"He was scared. I've studied those grounds many times. The sun was setting and Anna and I were in an area called the Peach Orchard taking pictures and trying to capture orbs. I was getting cold so I told Anna I was going back to the car. She asked me where I was and I waved to her until she faced me. As soon as she did, I saw a soldier appear, run across the field to the right and disappear. It was as clear as anything. I could tell the type of hat he wore, and his uniform. I just think of him running scared over and over for a hundred and fifty years."

"That's awful."

"The only other time I saw a full apparition was the night of Anna's accident. The other driver was killed. As they carried him away in a body bag on a gurney, I saw him sitting in the bed of the truck. He was crying until he lifted his head, looked directly at me and said he was sorry."

"Wow, Toby, you never told me that."

"Anyway, he was like Sara; he never left. The timing was right and it was the only thing that made sense. Instead of staying behind, like Sara did, he must have somehow possessed the box."

"Is that common?"

"I can't say how common it is, but there are many stories of ghosts haunting antiques, toys, and dolls."

She stared at me with a hint of a smile. I could see her out of the corner of my eye.

"What?"

She reached over and rubbed the back of her hand across my cheek, "You look like shit."

"Thanks, baby," I said with a laugh.

"Come on, let's get you cleaned up."

Later that day, we went to the hospital to make sure her ribs weren't broken. We told the doctor that she tripped and fell into an iron-backed chair. He bought the story, took some x-rays and sent us on our way with an elastic wrap for her to use. It helped restrict movement, but the only thing that could be done medically was to wait it out and control the pain with aspirin.

We spent most days together, but some we didn't. She had her appointments, I had my chores. I finalized the photographs I took that rainy day and spent a lot of my time writing.

There were no signs of Sara anywhere. I didn't hear any sounds, I didn't feel any cold chills and the only time I heard her voice was in my head. I knew Alex thought of her but didn't say anything until one particular morning, when she put some clothes in the closet and asked about the box on the floor. I knew exactly what she was asking about, but needed to think fast, so I asked her, "What box?"

"The one on the floor in here in the right-side closet."

I walked into the room thinking of how to reply to her and decided the truth would be the best.

"That's the dowsing rods, crystal and spirit box."

She looked at me intently without saying a word.

"What are you thinking, Alex?"

Her eyes began to tear up and she said, "I miss her, Toby. I was so mad at her for what she did to me, but it wasn't her at all."

"How do you know that?"

"I just know—will you show me—please?"

"Look, I miss her too. I really do. I'm just not sure I'm ready for that."

She closed the closet door as her tears began to fall. I hated to see her like that and I felt as though I had to put my own emotions aside for her.

"What the hell, bring the box out here."

"Really?" she smiled.

"Yeah, of course."

She reached down for the box, carried it to the dining room and set it on the table. Her excitement showed through fidgeting and smiles. I opened the box and pulled out all three instruments, setting each one on the table.

"Teach me," she said.

I handed her the dowsing rods first and I held the end of the chain in my fingertips until the dangling crystal stopped completely. Admittedly, I was nervous to know if someone was in there with us. What if someone was? And what if it wasn't Sara?

Alex began, "Is there anyone—"

"No," I interrupted. "We're looking specifically for Sara. Address only her."

She walked into the kitchen. "Sara? Are you here?"

I stood by the doorway to the spare bedroom and called out, "Sara."

I stared at the end of the crystal, occasionally looking up at Alex. Her eyes were focused intently on the ends of the brass rods.

I moved around the house slowly, whispering, "You know what to do. Just let us know you're here."

I reached the end of the galley kitchen by the doorway to the basement and tried again.

"Should I move around?" she asked.

"She knows about the rods. She'll come to you."

I walked over to the table and turned on the spirit box so she had three ways to let us know of her presence, then stood by the sliding door, holding the crystal still again.

"Maybe we should switch," she suggested.

I walked over to her, handed her the crystal and took the rods back by the glass doors.

"Sissy, please. I miss you so much. Where are you?"

After several attempts, she put the crystal in her hand and walked over to me crying. I set the rods on the table and held her. "I'm so sorry, Alex."

"She's gone, isn't she?"

Without her knowing, I slowly pulled my hand up to wipe tears away from my own eyes, then sniffled.

"You better not be crying too," she said.

I laughed and pulled away from her, both of us looking into each other's sad eyes.

"I can't help it," I said and wiped tears away. "It just seems so final."

"How do you think I feel? I have to say goodbye to her twice."

I reached over to turn off the spirit box.

"Wait. Not yet."

She picked up the box and held it tightly. "Goodbye, Sissy. I will always love you."

She held it close to her for a while until I reached for it and she slowly let it go. I turned the knob on the top and listened as the volume of the static lowered until it finally clicked off and I whispered, "Goodbye, Sara."

I put the instruments back into the box and closed it. I took it back to the closet while Alex sat at the table in tears.

"Are you hungry?" I asked. "Come on, I'll cook up some breakfast.

She nodded her head silently and I got everything out to make breakfast. I put on some light music and opened the blinds. The sun was hot already. It was a beautiful morning.

Bacon sizzled in the pan when a slow song came on and I walked over to Alex. I reached my hand out to her and helped her up, then guided her to the middle of the living room. My left hand held her right and our opposite hands were on our waists as we danced slowly and gracefully. When the song was finished, I guided her to the kitchen with me. I flipped the bacon over, then cracked some eggs into a mixing bowl. We both sang along to the next song; more to each other than just singing into the air.

I lifted her up to sit on the counter and poured the mixed eggs into the hot pan. As they heated up, I became mesmerized by the contents of the pan. My mind blocked out all sounds as I stared at the bubbling eggs. My trance was broken and Alex gasped when I shivered.

"Sara?"

◆

THE GHOST BETWEEN US

PETE NUNWEILER

Connect with me on social media for announcements
of Book 2, The Ghost Beside Us

Acknowledgements

Kris, you did it again. You believed I could accomplish something that I never imagined I'd even try; then you made me believe it. Thank you for being my biggest fan (I think Mom will be okay passing the torch to you now).

To Maryann, my Mother-in-law, as one of my test subjects, you got an early full copy of the book prior to editing. Your feedback and pride in me has made me genuinely proud of myself. Thank you for always supporting me.

Rob Williams at www.ilovemycover.com, you designed an amazing cover. I told you I wanted a cover designed early to build excitement for the book long before I finished writing it and you did that very thing. Thank you. You'll hear from me again for The Ghost Beside Us.

To Laura, the best editor a guy could ask for. You have a way with turning good to great. Thank you for the kind words during the process. You certainly made me feel amazing.

To my Facebook fans, especially Marie Atwell-Shoffner, for your genuine excitement when you read the Friday night previews, and Jenny Lesko for establishing the Ghost Between Us family by greeting each additional hundredth fan. Also, to my Dad, Marti Sholty, and Kim Wyckoff for sharing nearly every update and preview I posted.

Finally, I wouldn't be who I am without the people and experiences that have shaped me, including many captured in these pages. This appreciation goes to the friends who were there when Toby left his home. To the real Doug and Linda, you're thought of often. To the meat department kid behind the store, did you ever think back then that you'd be a published author? We did it, kid. I sure wish we would have believed in ourselves back then.

About the Author

Pete Nunweiler is an Army veteran who served as a cannon crewmember in the Third Armored Cavalry Regiment in El Paso, Texas from 1992–1994. After his Army experience, he continued to serve as a citizen soldier in the Indiana National Guard through 2002 as a Nuclear, Biological, and Chemical Warfare Non-Commissioned Officer.

He and his wife, Kris, are avid landscape photographers, specializing in waterfalls and cascades, primarily in The Great Smoky Mountains and the surrounding area. As a colorblind photographer, in 2014, along with Kris, they advanced their hobby into an online business under the name Nunweiler Photography. Their art can be found at www.nunweilerphotography.com.

Pete is an Eagle Scout from Troop 18 in the North Star District of the Crossroads of America Council of the Boy Scouts of America and continues to contribute to the Boy Scouts. In 1998, Pete was recognized as one of the top service providers in his company of 12,000 employees and considers that to be his greatest recognition. Pete is originally from the village of Springville, New York.

Other Books by Pete Nunweiler

One Hundred Seventy Days – A Caregiver's Memoir of Cancer and Necrotizing Fasciitis.

A mother is taken to the emergency room where she's seen by a doctor for the first time in forty-two years. What started as a simple procedure has escalated into a deadly situation. Her strength and her family's bond are tested when she is taken into one surgery after another. As her medical representative, the youngest son is faced with making crucial decisions that will determine her survival. When he receives the shocking news of the existence of a tumor, his options become extremely limited and the family is thrust into an emotional roller coaster.

One Hundred Seventy Days is the powerful true story of the unwavering strength of a woman and the indivisible bond of her family.

How Much Water Do We Have?: 5 Success Principles for Conquering any Challenge and Thriving in Times of Change

Do you have the 5 waters of success? Information, Planning, Motivation, Support, and Leadership. These essential elements will empower you to conquer any challenge and thrive in times of change. **How Much Water Do We Have?** *equips you to recognize the signs of dehydration at work and at home. You'll learn how to find, acquire, and use the 5 Waters of Success – and how to share them with your team and family members. Are you thirsty? Dive in!*

@5WatersBook, #5Waters

Published by Dave Burgess Consulting, Inc.